THE SEA PILOT

By
Donald L. Boone

BEFORE

RICHARD HUMPHRY

Richard Humphry was courting Constance Persing, and she wanted to know more about him than those in his newly found business community. He'd just purchased his second packet ship, and had opened an office down on the waterfront. It was at a social gathering of monied families that he'd met her. Richard had been invited to attend by her uncle, who saw Richard as a rising star in the shipping business. He had a charismatic way with people that opened doors for him that were not open to most others. It was during the social gathering that the two of them were engaged in a more personal conversation.

"Richard, why is it you became a businessman in the maritime trade, rather than a ship's Captain like your father and grandfather?"

He didn't want to tell her the real reason, "Some men are born to the sea, I'm not one of them. I enjoy the banter of bargaining, the haggling over prices. I enjoy the sea, but I enjoy the business end of it as well."

"My uncle thinks you have a natural gift for business and that you are well liked and respected. He expects you to become a wealthy man in a short time. And, I must say, with you owning two ships already, I am impressed."

Constance's family had money, and she never wanted for anything. She wasn't interested in Richard because of his potential, though her family was. She liked him because he looked out for others less fortunate than himself. He helped them get started when they had no other way to turn and he hired the common man. His mother had instilled consideration for others in him as he grew, and he believed in helping others better themselves.

"I tried the life of a man of the sea for a while, it simply didn't appeal to me."

"Richard, I must confess. I spoke with one of the men who works for my father. He knows you and your family. He told me that you always got violently seasick, and couldn't do your work aboard a ship." When she finished saying this to him, a wide smile spread across her face. She had him, and they both knew it.

He couldn't avoid the truth now. "Well, there was that as well."

IAN HAWKINS

As a child Ian was never one to play by the rules, he devised his own way of doing things. Because of his competing attitude, that and the fact that he raised the hackles on everyone who knew him, he was sent off to school. In the academy he excelled in strategic manipulations of those around him, resulting in his getting excellent grades. If left on his own, he might have failed. He became a member of Her Majesties Navy, and soon gained a reputation among the Admiralty staff, as someone who had an uncanny sense of how to attack the enemies of the crown, with little or no loss of his own, though he did not truly enjoy the military lifestyle.

He tired of the military rules, and against the wishes of many, he joined private enterprise, primarily to spend more time in less dangerous waters. The regimented ways of Her Majesties Navy, and war simply overwhelmed him. He could not see spending his life, taking the lives of others. When he met Richard Humphry, and was offered a position as a ship's Captain with a good wage, and a percentage of the profit from each voyage, he simply couldn't refuse. He quickly resigned his military officer's commission in her Majesties Navy.

JOHN DAVIS

He was tired, very tired. He'd only stopped long enough to check on a woman someone had said was in the building. He searched through the rooms vacated by the sick and dying until he found her. Dim light from the only window revealed a drab existence. Walls that may have never seen paint of any kind, a cooking pot on a long dead fire in her fireplace smelled putrid. Whatever she had attempted to make into a stew, long ago soured with age.

The physician sat on a hard stool by her bedside, bed clothing pulled up tightly about her neck in an attempt to keep some resemblance of warmth close to her wasting body. He felt her neck first then her wrist for a sign of her pulse. Even as his fingers probed her frail skin he knew it didn't make any difference, she was being taken like the others. Still, he listened to her as she rambled on about her boy. He didn't really care what it was she had to say, he was just too tired to get up at the moment. She too, was weak, her voice barely audible.

"He was always underfoot, e'was. You'da thought somethin' wrong with'im. Walkin' and talkin'. Always walkin' an talkin'. Jabberin' on things I had no such idea about. His father just didn't come home one day." She coughed some more.

"Where's the boy now?" He hadn't seen a boy's body about the place.

4

"Oh, I've no idea. John went to sea as a cabin boy years back. He's come up some since then, though. Dunno what he's'a doin' nowadays. Still at sea I speck."

"So, he's a seaman then?"

"Yes. Yes he is. He's been gone for two years come this Janu. . . ."

He looked up, her eyes were still open, but she was gone. He'd mark the door outside. The Cholera was taking them by the tens in this neighborhood alone.

JIM BARNSTABLE

He smiled to himself as he finished the last of a pipe full of tobacco. He'd been watching and listening to his wife, Maggie, plunking the things down on the table as she got their evening meal ready. She'd been fretting for days over their boy, Jim, and the latest news.

He tapped the last of the embers out of the pipe bowl into the fireplace, when she called to him, "Caleb. Your suppers gettin' cold."

She'd just set it on the table so it wasn't really getting cold yet. She was just fretting some more. "I'm'a comin', Maggie."

Maggie had wanted their son to do well. She'd goaded Caleb into getting the boy apprenticed to a Pilot, and he'd found one of the best. In the past he'd taken Jim with him on several voyages and he knew the boy was a smart one, this one. Had an interest in how stars worked, and how his Pa knew where they were while at sea. He'd shown the boy everything he himself knew, but that wasn't enough to satisfy his young mind.

He sat at his usual place at the end of the table, his plate already filled with a stew. Then his wife sat near him, speaking as she did so, "I'm tellin' you, it's not proper."

Caleb was well aware of what she was carrying on about, but innocently he said, "What's not proper?"

"Jim and that woman. You know very well what I'm talking about Caleb Barnstable. Don't you play that game with me."

"She seems a fine woman to me."

"She's a widow woman, and barely so. And, the two of'em are carryin' on as if they were wed."

"Now Maggie, don't fret so over this. Jim's a fine man, he'll do right by her. You know he will."

"Hummph. We'll see. We'll just see."

DANIEL MATHEWS

As someone who knew how to play chess, but who rarely had the chance, he decided to carve the pieces for a chess set to fill his empty hours at sea. He'd been carving other sets, but these were special and he'd been working on them for more than two years now. In his mind he remembered each piece and the detail he had put into them. It was as if he'd carved it only the day before. Ivory, though costly, brought him higher prices for his carvings on the wharf market, so he used it as much as he could. This chess set was to be entirely of the best Ivory.

Daniel kept a short, but very sharp knife in a sheath on his belt, and whatever piece he was currently working on, in his jacket pocket. While the crew followed the orders, given by himself, he had little to do, other than observe that things were getting done. To while away the time, he carved. John Davis, the First Mate happened by him late one day while he was working on the intricacies of a chess piece during his watch.

The mate had come up behind him, and had said, "What's that you're working on, Mister Mathews?"

Caught unawares, he simply handed the piece to the mate, "A Chessman, Sir."

"It's not very large, it must be a Pawn?"

The comment told Daniel, that the mate knew of the game. "Aye, Sir. I've carved the royal pieces and still have the pawns to finish."

"Does it take long? To carve these I mean?"

"It can, Sir. I only work on them to fill the empty time, like now, Sir. The crew's busy with their work, and I've only to see they do it proper. This gives me a few minutes to do something with my hands, Sir."

"I know your watch always gets their work done, I don't mind your carving as long as the ship is run right."

"Aye, Sir, and thank you, Sir."

The mate handed the piece back, saying, "I'd like to see the others sometime."

"Aye, Sir. I'll see that you do, Sir."

Daniel glanced at the Pawn in his scarred hand again, and his mind found the mental images of the other pieces. The Kings were represented by ship's Captains, The Queens were mermaids, the Bishops were represented by the ship's First Mates, the Knights were made in the form of men carrying the load of running the ship, the ship's Bosuns. The Rooks were capstans, and now, one by one, he was completing the Pawns. Each one different, but with a similarity so the eyes would know which side they belonged to. Each of them bore the form of different seamen he'd met and worked with over the years.

*   *

As was common the seamen from different ships took up positions to show their wares for sale on the wharf a day or two after each voyage ended. Some had gathered things from their different ports of call, but on this day Daniel was to meet Mister Humphry. John Davis had brought him by Daniel's chosen spot on the wharf.

He introduced the two men, then left them to talk while he took his wife, Rebeka, and the children, on to look at other things for sale in the seaman's market.

"I understand you carve chess pieces, Mister Mathews?"

Daniel was nervous. This man owned the very ships he sailed on, a man of influence and a man of money. "Aye, Sir. I do, Sir. Would you like to see them, Sir?"

"I would indeed, if you would be so kind?"

As Daniel opened a well-worn sea chest, and handed the pieces across to Richard, one at a time, so he could examine them thoroughly, he watched the wealthy man's eyes. They sparkled with glee.

10

"Am I too assume you're you going to sell these pieces?"

He'd already decided he would have no way to keep them safe himself, so he'd made the decision to sell them. "Aye, Sir. I will part with them Sir, but I've yet to finish the whole of them, Sir."

"Have you settled on a price yet?"

Daniel had thought long and hard about the time he had been working on the pieces, even though the time was in fragments, he still had an idea of how long it had taken him. He tried to figure how much he would have made in wages for that time, then took a chance by increasing the amount. The price he quoted he, himself, thought too high.

Mister Humphry surprised him. "I'll give you double that if I can have the ones you have finished now, and if you finish the others."

Daniel delivered the finished pieces to Richard's office the next day, and received gold coins for his payment. At the moment he was a wealthy man. He promised to deliver the pieces as he finished each of them. With that mind set, he took extra pains to make sure his work was perfect.

THOMAS FRANKLIN

The rain blinded the three men on horseback and their rain slickers flapped up into their view of the road before them. As the carriage came into view the leader said to the others, "It be here lads. Take care. They will be armed, so protect yourselves."

The youngest member of the three highwaymen, carried two black powder pistols, one in each hand. He was nervous, scared, and trigger happy. "What do we do if they start shooting at us?"

"You sit tight right there, Lad. We'll have them get out on your side. You watch'em close like. If they start to shoot, you kill'em right off." He was sure the kid would not be able to pull the trigger on anything, let alone hit anything with a pistol ball.

Two of them, astride their horses in the middle of the road, raised their hands in the pouring rain, the Lad off to one side. The driver of the carriage hired by Mister and Missus Franklin, saw the two men and thought them to be in some kind of trouble, so he stopped mid road. Then he heard the orders from the biggest of them to dismount. He turned toward the occupants of his carriage and said, "I think they mean to rob us, Sir."

Benjamin Franklin said, "Nonsense." He pulled his parasol to his lap and started to get out of the carriage. His wife, Marian, followed close behind, she more curious than anything else. The baby was asleep in a basket on the floor.

When the two of them started down the steps while departing the carriage interior, Benjamin began to open his parasol, the end of it pointing in the direction of the youngest bandit. He raised his pistol and fired, his aim true to its mark. Marian, her hair pulled back tight, rushed to her husband. Her parasol, too, unopened, looked like a long pistol. It too drew fire from the remaining pistol in the hands of the man on horseback nearest them.

After reining his horse in, he rushed around to the side of the carriage. The older man said, "What have ya done, Lad?"

"They were going to shoot me, so I fired first like you said."

During the melee, the driver ran off into the brush. As the three men looked at the dead couple, the rain let up enough for them to see the weapons they had pointed were but parasols. Then, they heard the cows being herded close by, and shouts from more than one voice. "Come lads, this is not the carriage we wanted. This be needless killin'."

As the man and his young daughter came over the rise, they found the grisly scene. As the farmer looked around, he heard the cry of a babe. He opened the carriage door and reached for the basket.

With it in his hands and a quick look, he gave it to his daughter. "You take the young'un on home. I'll be along soon's I put these folks to rest.

After he placed the couple in a shallow grave off to the side of the road, he went through their meager belongings. He couldn't read well, but the letter he found had a name from a place just a few miles distant. He'd take the child there in a day or two.

He turned the horses loose, then headed home. Shortly after he'd gone, the driver returned. He found only the empty carriage, the horses feeding nearby, and no one in sight. Bewildered by the whole event, he hitched up the team and returned to his own stable, not knowing the outcome.

Young Tom would have perished had it not been for the farmer and his young daughter who tended a small herd of milk cows and, by chance, had come upon the carnage. The letter found among the clothing led to his being delivered into the care of his grandparents. He was too young to remember the events of the incident, but that was really the beginning of his life.

Those early years were spent helping run the farm and, quite often, giving his grandmother a helping hand in the kitchen where she baked goods for sale in the public market. She and her husband raised him as best they could, going to church and teaching him manners. Not an educated woman herself, she had some basic understanding and taught him his numbers and letters. As he grew, he heard stories of the sea and it beckoned to him. His first ship was to be the Quest.

ONE

A January icicle broke loose and fell to the ground in front of Ian just as he reached for the office door of Humphry Shipping Limited. He'd been commanding Richard's ships for several years, but lately the shipping business had been less profitable than desirable. Richard's secretary, Martin, had come to he and Margaret's home earlier in the day to personally deliver a written message that Richard would like to see him as soon as it was convenient. He'd not been in at the time, but Jesselyn, Margaret's maid, had taken the message. The note briefly asked him to stop by the company's office, but Ian feared that with the lack of a profitable shipping season he was about to find his duties as a ship's captain, dramatically reduced. Though known to be one of the best ship's captains in this part of England, he was aging, and his health was no longer what it should be for the often harsh conditions found at sea.

When Ian entered the outer office he was met with the warmth of a fire in a central fireplace and the secretary, Martin, a man who seemed much to thin to be healthy and exhibited skin barnacles and liver spots as old age crept up on him. Martin was working quietly at his desk but rose to greet Martin when he closed the door behind him. "Good of you to come, Sir. This way if you will, Sir." Ian followed him to the private office at the back of the building. They stopped as Martin knocked at the door to his employer's office, opened the door slightly and stuck his head in, "Mister Humphry, Captain Hawkins is here, Sir."

From behind Martin, Ian heard the response, "Let him in, man. Let him in."

Martin closed the door behind him after he'd entered the inner office where he received a warm greeting, "Ian, nice of you to come. Can I get you some tea?"

He responded with, "Please." The greeting from Richard seemed quite cordial. There was no indication of it being a tight business meeting or as if there were any problems to be dealt with, so Ian began to relax. The office was well organized, one wall covered in books, mostly about the shipping business, and with volumes covering the trade routes of the world. A large world chart adorned another wall. The chart had notes and sketches added to various coast lines as new areas were being discovered. Carpets from China covered the floors. An intricately hand-carved desk from Japan took up most of the room in front of a large window overlooking the bay. The frosted panes restricted the view to small clear areas of each piece of glass.

After pouring each of them a mug of tea, Richard got right to the point. "Have you been aboard the *Quest* since the yard crews finished with her recent hull modifications?"

"Yes I have, though she's not in my command." His previous ship, the good ship Celeste, was now hauled out on the hard at the yard and undergoing extensive refitting. "It was a curiosity that drew me to board her and have a look around. I see you had two portals added aft, one in each of the small cabins aft of the gun deck. And some workmen were building some kind of large containers in the ship's hold."

"Yes, of one the new cabins, is to be for your First Mate, and one for the Sea Pilot I've employed. The main aft cabin will, of course, be yours."

Ian paused. His hand stopped the cup just before it touched his lips. "My First Mate, and . . . my cabin?"

"Yes, Ian . . . It is my wish that you will take her under your command."

This news came as a total surprise to Ian. He knew the Quest did not have a ship's Captain assigned to her and, though well qualified, he didn't expect to be given command of the largest Barque in the Humphry's company fleet.

Richard continued, "Before you answer, I must make sure you are aware of her next journey as it may be trying. You see, I want to take advantage of the current taxes before they are changed with the naming of Prince Charles as King. I propose a voyage to Madeira for a cargo of wines, then on to The West Indies for spices."

As an active ship's Captain, Ian said, "That's not the usual voyage, Richard. I would expect you to send a ship to Madeira for the wine, and another ship to the West Indies."

"That is the way I would normally arrange to have it done. But with the Celeste in the yard for work that will take some time to complete, and because our other ships will not be home until after the new year, I'm going to gamble on one ship doing both, as time is of the essence. Doing so in this manner will only require the expense of one ship at sea, over the expenses of two, and with a full cargo in her hold."

"It will take longer than a straight trip across to the Islands and back. Will the wines keep for an extended voyage of this length?"

"Did you look closely at the three large tanks built into the hold?"

"I did, and they didn't seem finished. Even after viewing them I still don't understand their use."

"They are to have a clay liner between the inner and outer shells of each tank. Two of them are to be filled with ice from the winter river, and covered with wood shavings to keep it from melting quickly. It's a gamble, but the ice should keep the wines chilled after you load them and, I believe, will keep them safe from the heat for the remainder of your voyage."

Ian dropped his head to his chest, his hand coming up to hold his chin as he thought about the prospect of the trip. It could produce a grand profit if the timing was right. "Richard, that is a clever idea. It should work and, Richard, the Quest is a beautiful ship. It would please me to have her in my command."

"Excellent. I'll have the Pilot go aboard after you've taken command, and he will have a helmsman with him."

"You're providing a Pilot and a helmsman?"

"Yes, though I expect you to continue with your own navigation, I would advise that you keep an open mind to Mister Becker's suggestions. He is quite inventive, and I've learned he has an excellent reputation. As you know, news travels from ship owner to ship owner, good or bad."

"It seems odd of you to employ a Pilot for one of your ships."

"Yes, it's an unusual arrangement but one I'm interested in trying out as I'm considering placing Pilots on each of our ships in the future. Not every ship's Captain can navigate well enough to make the fast passages needed these days."

"As you wish, Richard." Ian smiled. Margaret would be very pleased. This would mean a substantial increase in their income, and of her social standing.

TWO ☆

William had fussed for days over the selection of tools and charts he planned on taking along on this voyage. There was no need to take every navigational tool he'd acquired over the years, only the ones he thought he might need on this particular voyage. Each item in his inventory was, to him, a personal pleasure.

Such as his new Astrolabe for taking sights on the Sun, Moon, Venus, and other known planets. These tools were used to find his position on the surface of the Earth. The charts he had, he'd found during his travels to Spain and Portugal, each a treasure in itself.

He smiled again about his latest and most treasured find, a copy of Johann Werner's book of the Lunar tables, a Published Translation of Ptolemy's Geography. He marveled at such a simple method for finding the longitude by using the known speed of the moon and its diameter. He'd ordered a second copy and he'd give it as a gift after it's arrival.

His apprentice, Jim Barnstable, had started late to study navigation. He remembered that he himself had started when he was but eleven years of age. His own father, a ship's Captain, had by then taught him the basics of navigation. This had only been the spark to drive him with an obsession, his need of being able to find his location on the

Earth. In his early years he'd found that most ship's Captains considered a floating needle pointing a direction to follow, was evil. In many cases, the compass was hidden away and out of sight to most crewmen. Once he'd found out about the use of stars and planets to find the path around the Earth, everything else in his life had been forsaken in the quest for knowledge.

Even Beth had been lost to him. She'd simply tired of the wait and married a man who was home all the time. He couldn't help himself, his travels and studies ruled his life.

Finally, when he had his instruments ready, he had the driver help him load his things into the carriage, then they'd started off to the docks. As he rode in silence, hearing only the horse's hooves on the roadway, he glanced ahead and saw the couple in front of the carriage, they were but a short distance ahead.

"There, driver, just ahead. The sweeting couple. Drive slow as we pass them."

As Jim Barnstable walked slowly with Katherine so as to take pleasure in her being with him, her arm through his own, they spoke of their plans on his return from the sea.

They heard the open carriage as it came close, then he heard William's voice, "Jim, would the two of you like a ride the rest of the way to the Quest?"

Turning toward the carriage, Jim replied, "Thanking you William, but no. It's so close now. We'll walk the rest of the way."

"I'll see you aboard then." William smiled and tipped his hat to the woman with Jim as he continued speaking, "Miss Katherine, nice to see you once again."
"And you, Sir."

William spoke, "Driver, onward."

As Katherine watched the carriage disappear around a building just ahead, she thought about Mister Becker. He kept rooms just minutes from the waterfront where he lived alone. He'd never married, and did not have a sweetheart, as best she knew. "Is he a lonely man, Jim?"

"I don't think so. He always has a book in his hands. He studies every waking hour, he is a man of unusual knowledge, and seems possessed to learn more."

"How is it you became his apprentice?"

"A few years ago, my father made the arrangement for me. He knew of my interests and spoke to Mister Becker on my behalf. Father knew that Pilots can ask a large sum for their services, and I feel the coming years will be profitable for me. If I'm to make a living from the sea, this is the way I'd like to do it."

"How much longer will it take to start making your living as a Pilot?"

"I've learned much already. Another trip, maybe two, and I may apply for my first ship as a Pilot. I wanted to go aboard the Quest as a second Pilot, but Mister Humphry said he'd not pay the wages of two pilots. He did offer me a position aboard as a helmsman. Of course I'll have to serve aboard as an able-bodied seaman as well, but I'll be aboard with William."

"I trust that you will be learning more from him on this voyage?"

"We will work together as much as our time aboard allows."

"I understand, from your talks with Mister Becker, that this is to be a fast voyage."

"Aye, it is. And on my return, Love, we will find a Priest, if you're still of that mind."

She squeezed his arm, then reached up to kiss him on the cheek. "Thank you, Jim. I'll be a good wife to you."

He was sure she would be a good wife. He was sweet on her, she liked being in bed with him, and she could cook, and kept their rooms sparkling; what more could a man want.

THREE ✭

"You sent for me, Captain?"

"Yes, John. . . . I understand the Pilot is aboard?"

"Yes, Sir, and he chose the small starboard gun cabin, Sir."

"And yourself?"

"I've taken the liberty of moving my duffle into the port gun cabin, Sir."

"Very well, and the Helmsman?"

"Forward, Sir. In the fo'c'sle with the rest of the crew."

"Very good, now, if you will muster the crew, John."

"Aye, Sir." The two men went topside to the bridgedeck and the First Mate called out, "Mister Mathews, Mister Rankin, muster the crew."

The two Bosuns spread the word, and the ship's crew assembled aft of the main mast, standing just to the rear of the cook shack, and below the bridgedeck rail. Both Bosun's Mates counted the men in their watch section and reported, "All hands present, Sir."

The First Mate, John Davis, was strongly built. He was the kind of man women fantasize about, his arms straining at the sleeves as muscles rippled, his chest full and covered in dark hair. He had already chosen his words for this first meeting with the crew. He had no intention of telling them that they already had a cargo of ice on board. The hold was locked and only he and the Captain had the means to enter there.

The Captain and the Pilot stood aft of John Davis, each overlooking the proceedings about to take place. The First Mate quickly looked over the crew himself, counting as he went. He was making certain there was one extra man aboard. "You men may already know, but for those who don't, this is to be a faster voyage than normal. We will load cargo in Madeira, then cross to The West Indies. There will be little time in Ports of Call to squander and the amount of time you will have to spend on the beach will be short."

He looked about him, then continued with, "Now a word from the Captain."

Ian stepped to the bridgedeck rail and unrolled a sheath of papers. "I'm to read the ships articles to you."

As he started, he noticed the men were already restless. Most had heard these rules of the ship so many times they probably knew them by heart. It took him a quarter hour to finish. He was also aware that every man aboard had signed a copy of the ship's articles. The enforcement of the rules aboard was often left up to the ship's Captain's discretion, and was carried out by the ship's Mates or the Captain himself.

These shipboard rules form a bondage each man agrees to abide by. Each man aboard also understood, no matter his station, that any wrong committed by a man in the fo'c'sle against another crew member, would be handled amongst them; often brutally.

The Captain's last statement was unnecessary, but he finished with, "You should know that anyone who fails to obey orders will be punished accordingly. This is to be a fast voyage, so we will be driving the ship hard. Mind your footing when aloft, and. . . . if you take a fall overboard, we won't be stopping to save you. . . .Anyone have a question?"

The newest crewman, Tom Franklin, a willowy young man who would fill out as his life aboard demanded it, said, "Sir, if I may Sir, how long could a man live in this cold water, Sir?"

"Not long, Lad. It's bitter cold, it is. If you fall overboard, there is something you can do to put an end to your suffering, should you so choose."

All hands looked up, each wanting to know the answer to this question. "What would that be, Sir?"

"Keep a marlin spike with you at all times. Should you fall over the side, drive it through your eye." He smiled as he saw young Franklin shiver at the thought of killing himself in this manner. "Any thing else?" he asked.

Three Finger Jack had a question to ask, but knew it would not be answered. He'd found the hold locked, and he wanted to know why.

The men, tired of standing, were shuffling about on their feet when the First Mate said, "Mister Mathews, Mister Rankin, turn the crew to their chores."

FOUR ✲

Margaret Hawkins stood near her husband in his cabin. She liked his cabin and she was a part of it; the richness of the woods, the smell of her man, and that of the sea. She'd seen to it that he had a good quilt to keep him warm at night, and she had chosen his blankets carefully as well.

Now, though, his sea bed was taunting her; at times the two of them had fit on it nicely. "Ian, I miss you so when you're away. I need you at home in my arms and in my bed at night." She leaned toward him, her ample bosom showing cleavage. She was trying to entice him to take her before she had to leave the ship.

He liked the manner in which she teased him, but the tide was about to change and he would need more time than that available to take care of her needs. "I know you do, My Dear, and we may be in luck. This trip could bring us a small fortune from the Captain's share alone, and I've been promised a bonus if we make a fast trip. At least enough to allow me many months at home on my return, perhaps longer if we keep our spending under control."

A knock at the door to the Captain's cabin, brought them back to the ship's business. Ian hugged her close one more time, then said, "Come."

The First Mate, John Davis, poked his head in. "The tide has turned, Sir." He smiled when he saw Margaret. "Afternoon Missus Hawkins."

"Afternoon, John. John, you look after my husband, you hear?" She liked John. She knew him to be trustworthy and loyal to her husband. She did not like the fact that the spell had been broken between her and her husband, but it had.

"Yes, Mum. I surely will, Mum."

Ian looked at his wife of many years. "I'm sorry my dear. We have to cast off to catch the tide and the offshore breeze."

She kissed him fully on the lips, then, smiling at John she left the Captain's cabin and went ashore.

After Margaret Hawkins had seen her husband doff his cap to her from the bridgedeck, she'd seen the younger woman nearby wave to someone on board the Quest as it gathered way while leaving the wharf.

It was the woman's red hair that had drawn Margaret's attention in the beginning. Her own hair had been near that color when she was younger, though now it had darkened to near auburn with strands of grey beginning to show. She gathered her skirts to keep them dry and up out of the mud, then she turned toward the door of her waiting carriage. Before she boarded, she asked the driver. "Do you know of that woman? She's not familiar to me."

"Yes, Mum. She's the widow Wilson, Mum. Her husband went missing at sea last year."

The widow Wilson was apparently considering a new man in her life. "A widow you say? How does she get by?"

"She's one of Missus Bellis's hairdressers, Mum."

FIVE ⋆

The Sea Pilot, William Becker, heard the ships bell strike six times as he stood next to Captain Ian Hawkins at the port rail of the bridgedeck. He and the Captain each wore long coats to fend off the cool air coming in off the sea beyond the harbour this early April day. The crew, working the ship around them, did not notice the chill in the air the work keeping them warmed.

The Captain looked toward the masthead, then at the trees onshore surrounding the small towne of Still Water. Then his gaze crossed over the surface of the saltwater bay, it had turned from a flat oily finish to ripples on the surface. Satisfied with what he saw he spoke to the mate. "Mister Davis."

John Davis, the first mate stood to the port side of the massive hardwood wheel. The oak spokes, showing wear from a helmsman's hands, were worn through the polished coating down to bare wood. On the ship's helm this day stood one of the new men aboard, Jim Barnstable. The First Mate turned to acknowledge the Captain's summons, "Aye, Captain."

"Loose the ship. Take us to sea, Sir."

"Aye, aye, Sir." The mate's eyes quickly scanned the main weather deck below him, then he looked forward. Satisfied with his findings, he called out to the starboard watch Bo'sun. "Mister Rankin, away, Sir. Loose your lines to the wharf."

Raymond Rankin, a short stocky man whose skin showed years of abuse from the sun at sea, busied himself getting his crewmen to cast the mooring lines loose. Though the old hands understood what each of them were to do, he'd have to keep an eye on the newer men aboard. Old hands aboard, or new, they waited until the Bo'sun's mate gave them the order. As the lines were cast off the slight offshore breeze began to push against the bulk of the ship, and she eased away from the wharf. Shortly, he called aft to the First Mate saying, "We're away, Sir."

John Davis measured the distance between the ship and the wharf, then continued his orders to the Bo'sun. "Hoist the Flying and Outer Jibs, and the Spanker, Mister Rankin." He decided to leave the Inner Jib furled for the time, and the Mainsails would be readied soon enough. At the moment he had another matter to attend to first, one that would put a small measurement of fear into the minds of his crew.

"Aya aye, Sir. The Flying and Outer Jibs, and the Spanker, Sir."

In unison the first two Jibs were hoisted from where they lay bedded at the ready on the bowsprit. As they were made ready, the tops of each started their path upward to the masthead, the slight breeze filling each as they rose skyward. The lines from the foot of each sail were hauled in tight to trim the sail as it climbed up the forestay to which it was hanked. To the trained eye the Outer Jib seemed to be drawn tighter than the Flying Jib. To an experienced man of the sea there was no question it was not in proper trim.

Aft on the bridgedeck two men hoisted the gaff-rigged Spanker sail aloft just over the helmsman's head. The spars, freshly painted, gleamed in the sunlight, the loops around the mizzen mast rattling against the wood as the sail went up. Jim Barnstable never looked up. His eyes stayed focused on the distant entrance to the bay, a point of land they would clear soon enough. Then he glanced down to the compass binnacle to confirm his heading.

The Pilot had little to do at the time. His work would come in the days ahead. As he glanced toward the wharf, he saw two women standing there, one in a long, full, and expensive lacy white dress. A decorative parasol was shading her head, though her red hair seemed in some disarray as if blown by the sea breeze. A hired carriage waited for her nearby, the driver had his long coat pulled tightly about his body trying to keep warm on his high perch. The wealthier woman of the two waved to the Captain standing near him. His eyes also caught the movement as the Captain doffed his cap in return. He knew the younger woman on the wharf, dressed in meager clothing, and she waved as well. She also threw a kiss toward the ship. William looked forward to see the Helmsman's hand shoot high into the air. A wave of his hand signaled his goodbye to her. He had only learned recently that his apprentice had a woman beholden to him, not that it mattered.

"Mind your helm, Mister Barnstable."

"Aye, Sir," he said to the First Mate on his left.

John Davis did not let his eyes leave the ship, but he knew there was a woman on the hill watching the ship's departure through a looking glass. Had he looked, he might have seen the sun glint off the lens as the ship moved through her line of vision. He hated to leave her and the children behind, but this was his livelihood.

Just off the port bow, the lines of a small fishing skiff were cast loose from a low floating dock, and the woman at the oars started rowing. Her course seemed directed, as if to intercept the good ship Quest as it neared her. When she reached a position she had previously chosen, she rowed more slowly. She maintained what seemed like a controlled drift, a maneuver like a fisherman might use while trolling for an evening meal. No one paid notice of her as she waited. Her anticipation, known only to her at the moment, would soon be overtaken as adrenaline pumped through her veins.

As William stood near him, Captain Hawkins spoke quietly to the Mate. "Mister Davis."

As John turned to face the ship's Captain, Captain Ian Hawkins raised his right hand up to his left shoulder, a finger crooked to beckon the Mate to his side. When the Mate moved close, the Captain continued, "Seems we have an extra man aboard, do we not?"

"Aye, Sir. We do, Sir. I'll take care of that soon, Sir."

"Very well, Mister Davis."

Just as the ship was gathering way under her canvas, the First Mate called out to a member of the deck crew standing near the port rail. "Mister Rawlins, your Outer Jib is hauled tight. Ease her some."

The man handling the Outer Jib sheet, looked forward, then turned aft to face the Mate. "The Jib is drawing well, Sir." He turned away from John, and looked again at the Jib, but made no move to make any change in the sail trim. It was as if he was disregarding the orders of the man in charge.

John Davis, the First Mate bellowed, "What did you say, Mister Rawlins?" His booming voice carried the entire length of the ship's deck. Every man stopped to see what was angering the Mate. Those who had shipped with John before knew he was not a Mate to question. You did his bidding when he ordered it, and you did not speak back to him.

Mister Rawlins barely turned to acknowledge the Mate as he said, "I said, 'The Jib is drawing well, Sir.' It doesn't need to be trimmed, Sir."

In seconds John was down the bridgedeck steps, his feet hardly touching each of the wooden platforms, his hands guiding him as he slid down the well-polished hand rails. He moved forward with swift strides, his long legs covering the deck quickly. When he'd reached to where Mister Rawlins stood waiting, the Mate hoisted the man onto his shoulder and, after moving to the port rail, he threw him overboard. He watched long enough to see Rawlins head clear the water's surface, a fist raised in the air, an unheard curse aimed at the ship and the Mate.

The Mate, still appearing angered, turned to a young lad who just finished coiling a line to a topping lift at the foremast. He said, "You there, Franklin, is it?"

The lad was frightened. "Aye, Sir. Franklin, Sir."
His knees weakened as he waited the Mates next
words.

"Well, Mister Franklin, tend this Jib sheet and
ease the Jib to proper trim."

The lad hastened to the Mate's side to do his
bidding, nearly stumbling on the edge of the
ship's hatch cover. Though he stood before the
mate, he had not picked up the line to ease the
Jib sheet out. Instead, with down cast eyes, his
hands busy with each other, he said, "I'm beggin'
yer pardon, Sir, but I don't yet know my ropes,
Sir."

John Davis looked at the lad, but just for a split
second. *'The lad begged my pardon, he's been
fetched up proper.'* He broke his gaze with the lad,
his eyes searching for the Bo'sun. He found him
near the Capstan. "Mister Rankin, if you will."

In seconds the Bo'sun was at his side. "Teach the
lad how to trim the Jib sheets. It'll be his duty for
now."

"Aye aye, Sir. I was to start him on his ropes on
the morrow, Sir."

The Mate walked slowly aft as if inspecting
everything he passed, then up the steps to the
bridgedeck and to the Captain's side. "The ship's
company is now in proper trim, Sir." Then without

further word, he went to the highly varnished forward rail of the bridgedeck, this just ahead of the helm. As his eyes quickly scanned the ship's decks, a grin crossed his face, though briefly.

Other than the Bo'sun, and the lad Franklin, not a man had moved, each had been struck by what had just occurred. "Back to work!" he barked. Every man Jack began to find something to do, no matter if it needed to be done or not. Not a one of them wanted to be the next one thrown over the side.

The Pilot, William Becker, a slender man whose body indicated someone who made his living by using his mind rather than his physical strength, also awed by the event, spoke to the Captain, "Sir, the ship's company is now a man short, Sir."

"Not now, Mister Becker, not now. We'll speak of it later."

The Captain spoke to the Mate again, "Mister Davis."

As John turned, he said, "Aye, Sir."

"Once you've cleared land's end and set the sea watch, would you join Mister Becker and me in my cabin?"

"Aye, Sir."

The Captain turned his attention to William. "Mister Becker bring your charts and join me in my cabin at eight bells."

"Aye, Captain." William began to wonder what kind of men he was going to sea with.

SIX ✫

At the cherry wood writing desk in her bedroom, Margaret penned a quick note inviting Elizabeth for tea, then had her maid deliver it to the Bellis residence. They knew each other well enough not to stand on the proper etiquette most often practiced in their social circles. It was common for them to drop in on one another unannounced. Her maid Jesselyn, soon returned with an acceptance.

Within the hour the two women sat discussing the latest gossip around the towne. Elizabeth said, "I understand Ian has a new command?"

Proudly, Margaret answered, "Yes, he's taken command of the barque, Quest. She's the largest ship in Mister Humphry's fleet."

With a cup of tea held at the ready and soon to be lifted to her lips, she said, "I expect that means an increase for your household funds as well?"

"Yes, and a Captain's share of the profit from the cargo." Ian had told her she wasn't to spend good money until it was in their hands. He was a Captain at home as well. Fair, as with his ship's crews, he rules with a firm hand in both places.

"My, that is good news."

"He's to bring spices and Madeira wine home from this voyage."

After a lull in the conversation, Margaret mentioned, "Elizabeth, I'm in need of a hair dresser. Are you familiar with someone I might hire?"

Elizabeth sat up straighter, her eyes glancing at the ceiling, her mind searching for someone she might know. "Not really, but I can listen around if you like."

"Yes, if you will. Let me mention, however, I would prefer someone with hair of a red shade. You see, this would be a woman who understands the needs of my own hair." She reached up to fluff her hair, drawing attention to the color.

Elizabeth smiled. She felt there was more to it than just the reason given for this request. There was something about it that she didn't understand, but said, "I myself have such a hairdresser. . . .I could. . . .if you like. . . .I could part with her."

"Really! Would you mind if I take her into my employ?"

"Of course not, dear friend. I'll send her round in the morning."

"Thank you so much."

Elizabeth was not about to let a favor go freely, "Could you arrange for some nutmeg to find its way to me when your husband returns? It would be so nice to have some for the lockets I keep about my neck, so that I might freshen my breath. And of course for my husband's food and drink."

"Of course I will. I shall see that an ample amount will find its way to you."

After Elizabeth left, Margaret gave Jesselyn instructions to freshen the bedroom in the loft.

SEVEN ✶

She missed him already, and he'd not been gone long; still, she was without her man again. She had reservations before they were wed about spending her life with a man of the sea. She knew from the stories of the other wives around the wharf that their men were often gone for months on end. Sometimes it was years before they came home again, if they came home at all. Still, she'd found John's ways had enticed her to join with him. He seemed a hard man on the ship, but she knew him to be one of the kindest men she'd ever known. He had provided for her well, and he wasn't a man to squander his pay on grog and useless items.

One night, before this voyage began, and as he rested by her side having pleasured her and then himself with her. "Becky, need be, Mister Humphry will see to you, should your purse come short for coins to purchase what you need whilst I'm gone."

As was her habit, one learned from other wives of seafaring men, she always put some of his wages away just in case of a time of need. Now, however, she was more curious about the arrangements with the Shipping Company. "Will you be getting a Mate's share of this trip, like the last?"

He put his arm around her neck and pulled her tight to his side. Her breasts pushing into him, warming him again. "Aye, and we will get a larger share this time, if all goes well."

"How's this to be, John?"

"Ian told me that he'd had a talk with Mister Humphry and that with me as his trusted First Mate, and being as I'd served with him on other voyages, he felt I was to get a better share from this trip, as it is to be a fast voyage."

She smiled as she felt his enjoyment of her closeness begin, "Are you going to fool the crew this time too?"

He pulled her closer, "I'm going to try."

*   *   *

She'd kept an eye out for the morning breeze, waiting for it to fill in. Just then her eye caught the leaves on a tree near her window stirring. Instinctively she went to the mantle over the fireplace, picked up John's glass and moved to the window. Had she waited longer she might have missed seeing the ship just starting to make its way to sea.

Then remembering John's trick, she scanned the bay ahead. *'Yes, that would be her rowing out.'* They'd not met, but knew of each other. Then Rebeka's eyes returned to the ship her man was aboard, and the ache for him started again. "I love you John." escaped from her lips.

Two children, full of energy, came bursting through the door. They were hungry, of that she was sure, and her thoughts returned to her home, but the need for John remained.

EIGHT ★

The Quest, sailed outward bound with two Jibs, the Topsails, the Foresail, and Mainsail all set,had just cleared the end of the peninsula, and now had the starboard watch set. The port watch, standing down from the sea detail, could now rest until eight bells and their next turn on watch. The fishing skiff, having gone unnoticed, had hurriedly returned to its landing after the Quest had passed close by the small boat.

With the first sea watch set, the Mate gave the helmsman his sailing orders, though Jim already knew the route they would follow by heart. "Steer a Sou' by Sou' East course, Mister Barnstable." "Aye, Sir. Sou' by Sou' East it is, Sir."

"When we clear the light at Coverack, steer Sou' by Sou' West."

"That'll put the Lizard well off to our starboard, Sir."

"Aye, and that'll be a good course."

"Aye, Sir. The rocks at Lizard have taken many a good ship, Sir."

The Mate smiled as he said, "I'm to understand there are ghosts of men waiting nearby, men lost on the Lizard rocks. To warn or beckon, of which I'm not sure."

*   *   *

Jenny too, was chilled, but not nearly so much as her man. She'd rowed deeper into the bay as soon as the Quest took its leave of the area. She needed to hurry to help him out of the cold water. When she got to him he'd had the strength to pull himself aboard over the stern of the skiff, but barely. Even with a dry sail canvas about his shoulders he shivered uncontrollably from the cold. With him safely in the skiff she'd pulled with all her being, back to the floating dock from whence she'd come. He'd not had an attack in some time, but she was never sure when one might overtake him.

Her husband warmed himself close to the blazing fire in the fireplace. He no longer shivered, but still suffered from the cold. She'd bed him if he didn't warm soon, but she hadn't taken a chance of his warming slowly.

Jenny had used firewood instead of coals to bring more, and quicker, heat to the fire. Now he had a blanket wrapped tight about his shoulders, his wet clothes and boots shed inside the cottage door.

As she brewed him a hot broth, she thought about the extra money he'd earned this week. Five weeks wages for one weeks work.

He'd even told her she could have a few pence to spend on her own wants. Grateful she'd be for a new needle, and perhaps some pink thread she had seen in a shop in the towne.

NINE ✫

As William heard the ship's bell sound eight times, he had just finished selecting the items he planned on taking to the Captain's cabin with him. His personal compass was stowed in a safe place yet open to his view, but it would be left where it was resting at the time. The Astrolabe and the Compassum Meridianum for figuring deviation were both stowed properly as well. He'd also brought along a spare ship's log and lead line on this voyage and he would bring it to the Mate's attention when it could be shown properly. In his possession was a prized translated Mariner's Mirrour, published by Lucas Wagenaer, and it contained a Mariner's Atlas. For the moment he would only take his log book and the sheepskin charts he needed. The ship's hull rolled slightly as he made his way to the Captain's cabin door. A deeply carved mermaid, sitting on a harbour rock and blowing a conch shell, adorned the rich wood. He knocked once and heard the word, "Come."

Closing the intricately carved and polished wood door behind him, he moved into the cabin slowly. In his moment of waiting for the Captain to start the conversation, he became more aware of a man who was showing his age; his hair was graying, his stomach was beginning to bulge round, like that of a well-fed babe in his mother's arms.

"Ahh, William. Put your things on the table there. His fingers pointed to a large chart table to his left. Would you take a rum, or, I've sherry if you prefer."

"Sherry, if you please, Captain." He placed his things next to the Captain's ship's log on the table.

"Sherry it is then, and William, when you're present in my quarters by invitation, we go on first names. On the working deck we'll maintain the proper ship's protocol."

"Yes, Captain."

"Ian, William. It's Ian."

"Yes, Sir. Ian, Sir."

The Captain handed him a glass of sherry saying, "Make yourself comfortable. Try that chair," again he pointed. The chair had a cushion with red and pink roses embroidered into the cloth, no doubt provided by the Captain's wife.

After seating himself, the Captain continued, "William, I don't know how much you've been told about our journey, but I'll fill you in on what Richard Humphry expects of us."

William took the cue. "The ship's owner, Mister Humphry hired me to get you and this ship to Madeira, then across to the West Indies, and home again in the shortest time possible."

"And, the helmsman, Mister Barnstable?" Ian knew the helmsman had been requested by his ships Pilot.

"He's apprenticed to me by his father. Though he's signed aboard as an able-bodied seaman, I've been teaching him to be a ships Pilot for some time now."

"Hmm, I see. When I was in Richard's office, as of late, he gave me the responsibility of this ship, and of course her crew. His main concern, which is to be expected, is to make a profit from the voyage. He is more concerned now that Prince Charles is about to be named King. The Prince is a man bent on heavily taxing those who have it, and even taxing those who don't."

"Yes, so I've been informed, and I believe you are correct. He may be a threat to the financial well being of the business community."

"I've expressed my concerns to Richard about making a voyage in this manner, as it seems backwards for the cargo we seek. But then, you already know we've loaded a cargo of ice covered with wood shavings in clay lined tanks. The ice is to keep the wine from Madeira cooled for the remainder of the voyage home. Of course the crew does not yet know of the ice. If they did, it would disappear quickly in the lower latitudes and not from just the heat."

"Yes, I understand the river ice was delivered from the ice warehouse and brought aboard before I arrived. I know little about the preservation of wines, Ian. Will the ice last long enough?"

"I pray it will. It should. Some will melt of course, and the melt water will drain into the bilge, but we have to get the wine home as fast as we can. As Sea Pilot, how long do you expect our voyage to last before we reach home waters once again?"

"Of course, this will depend on the weather, and the ships crew. It is possible to make the trip in five or six months, possibly less, not counting the time spent in loading the cargo in each port, and I don't believe we can avoid some bad weather along the way. But, we are leaving at the best time of year to make the trip."

"I've not sailed with a Pilot before, I've always done my own navigating. However, I have no problem with your handling the navigation, of course I'll keep my own records as well. Richard asked that I consider any suggestions you might have as to navigation, and I will do that as well.

I understand you have a few new thoughts on the subject."

"Yes. I've come across some methods to help us better understand our speed, and our position each day. I also have, at a great expense to myself, the latest navigational tools and charts.

"I see you brought your charts along, and we can go over those. . . " There came a knock at the Captain's door, and the conversation came to a halt. "That will be John Davis." He turned to the door, "Come."

The First Mate opened the door. "You asked me aft, Sir."

"Yes, of course, John. You've met our Pilot, William Becker?"

"Yes, Sir." He stuck out his hand in a renewed gesture, and it was taken.

"How is it on deck, John?"

"We may get some weather, but we're about to round Coverack. I've given the order to steer Sou' by Sou' West as the wind is from the North. The port watch is on deck and, also, the Bo'sun Mathews."

"Very good. Help yourself to a rum, John"

"Thank you, Ian."

As John poured a mug of rum, Ian explained.

"William, John has served as my First Mate many times over the years. He gets the job done, and is of firm hand."

Smiling, William said, "I noticed his firm hand earlier, on deck."

Both Ian and John smiled at the remembrance of the earlier incident. "John, perhaps you should explain what happened."

The Mate smiled, set his mug down, and began. "You see William, rather than have to punish a man for insubordination or a few other wrong doings, I'd rather strike fear into their hearts in an easier manner. Though I can, and will, do what is required to maintain order aboard my ship. . .The man I threw overboard today, Mister Rawlins, was hired by me for just that purpose. I use him, and one other man, on occasion, to stage these kinds of events. I swear them to secrecy, and I pay them well."

William nodded, as he grinned. Now he understood. "That is a good trick. Does it work well?"

"Every time."

Ian spoke, "William you know of course, anything discussed in this cabin is not to be repeated elsewhere?"

"Agreed."

"Well then, let's get to the charts."
William spread his charts on the table and began the description of his planned routes around the great circle route. Just as he started his explanation, there came a knock at the Captain's door. Ian looked at both men, then called out, "Come."

As the door was opened, a seaman looked in saying, "Mister Mathews would like Mister Davis to join him on the bridgedeck, Sir."

John responded, "Tell him I'll be right along."

"Aye, Sir." and he pulled the door closed behind him.

Ian spoke up, "Well, then. We can take this up again in the next day or so."

William agreed, as did John, and their meeting was adjourned.

TEN ✭

On the bridgedeck the bo'sun, Daniel Mathews, came along side the First Mate saying, "Beggin' your pardon, Mister Davis, but we've a fresh crew and if you've some sailing orders for the coming weather. . .?"

"Aye, there is a blow comin' on. The winds are shifting to the South, and will likely go to the Sou', by Sou' West. We could be in for a rough night of it, Mister Mathews."

"Aye Sir, I believe so, Sir. My question to you, Sir, is with the coming heavy weather, do you want to carry full canvas and make some distance, or, shorten sail and ride easy like, Sir?"

"We should make a fast passage when we can and the ship is strong, her timbers sound." He smiled knowing the work that lay ahead, then said, "a green crew needs to learn about rough weather right away. Hoist all sail, Mister Mathews."

"Aye, Sir. With your permission, Sir, I'll see to it now while me crew is fresh."

"I'd say that's a good thing to get done straight away."

Rankin, the starboard watch Bo'sun was still standing on the bridgedeck, his watch having just been relieved. He offered, "You'll be wanting my men's help then?"

"Aye, we will need all hands," Mathews replied.

Mathews moved to the helm. "Mister Bowman, we've some weather coming aboard. Keep a close watch on your helm. We're going to carry all canvas. You may have to luff her up some on occasion."

"Aye aye, Sir."

While John Davis watched his Bo'sun give his orders, and the way his new crew responded, he could see a few errors being made by the raw crew. He'd have to spend some time with them to explain how he wanted things done so as to help the ship, and for the safety of each man aboard. But for the moment he was satisfied all would go well. "I'll be in my cabin if you need me, Mister Mathews."

"Aye, Sir. If'n I'm in need I'll send someone to fetch you, Sir"

John stood a few minutes more as the sails were un-furled and gaskets removed. The inner Jib joined the other two already at the masthead. Soon she would fly.

He took one last look around, then he retired to his cabin. He knew he'd better get some rest now, because he felt sure he'd be up later.

ELEVEN ☆

During the night a light rain began to fall, then the wind picked up and the earlier rain turned to a downpour that found every crevice in a man's clothing that could be flooded with water. In a short time the wind was howling through the rigging, some lines high aloft sang with a strumming heard only in rough weather.

The seas were building to new heights with each passing hour and the horizon disappeared from the view of the man at the helm as the ship reached the bottom of each trough. By now the ship's crew had put a reef in each of the Jibs and two reefs in the Spanker. Only the fore Mainsail, and the Mainsail were still set. The upper Topsails, and the lower Topsails were bunted up to the yards, their gaskets in place.

There was no need to carry full canvas any longer as the ship was moving fast through the water. Fast enough to concern the helmsman as he swung the wheel from side to side trying to keep the ship on a manageable course. For ships built like these, surfing down the front of a wave was terrifying. It took the courage of a skilled helmsman to handle her cranky ways.

At four bells he was already awake when the knock came at his door. "Aye."

The door opened slightly, "It's me, Sir. Seaman Samuel, Sir. Mister Mathews would like you to join him on the bridgedeck, Sir."

"Very well. Tell him I'll be along."

The ship was heeled over close hauled on a starboard tack, and even under her shortened sail she was surfing down the face of the shorter waves after the crest of a wave top passed under her keel. Seas often broke over the bow, running down the deck and out through the ample scuppers. As the First Mate reached the bridgedeck, the Bo'sun spoke loudly to be heard. "We've been making good time, Sir. We're going too fast for full sail, Sir. I don't know her speed, but I think she needs to be slowed with warps."

"You've a log man, that should give you her speed in knots."

"It's a fouled mess, Mister Davis. It's not reliable."

Something came to mind as the two men talked, and John said, "Send Seaman Samuel down to wake the Pilot and have him join us topside. And get someone to lend a hand to your helmsman." In less than ten minutes the Pilot, William, was at the side of the two men, and Seaman Samuel was taking orders from Mister Bowman on the wheel.

"She's tough to bring up, Lad. Just follow my lead and heave with all your might." Before the night was to end, Samuel would be exhausted.

John Davis was speaking, "Mister Becker, you told me a bit about a new log you brought aboard. Can it be used?"

William smiled. He was proud to have been asked. "Aye, we can for sure. I'll get it from my cabin."
When he returned, William explained the log to the First Mate and the Bo'sun, as he readied it to trail over the side. Both men agreed when he said, "You've probably not seen a ships log like this one before."

"You drop this end with the weighted circle of wood over the side. The three small lines form a crow's foot and connect to a longer line. The log line has knots spaced forty-eight feet apart. When it is dropped in the sea, you turn this small sand glass over and it runs for a half minute as the line pays out off the reel. When the glass runs out of sand, stop the line. Then as you pull it back in you count the knots that are out."

John said, "These knots you count as it is pulled back aboard gives us the ships speed then?"

"Aye, it's that easy."

They had the Bo'sun hold the reel of line as John dropped the disk overboard. When it hit the water, the Bo'sun felt it jerk in his hand. Immediately he turned the glass over and the sand began to run. When it ran out, he stopped the line from going further. As they watched, John counted the knots as the line was pulled aboard and wrapped back around the reel. When he'd finished, he said, "Mister Becker, if this is right, the ship is doing more than twelve knots!"

"That is her speed, Mister Davis, and if I might offer some advice?"

"If you will, Mister Becker."

"You're on a starboard tack. If you stay on this course, you'll make too much Easting."

John knew they were close to the Bay of Biscay. He hoped they were slightly to the south, but if the ship closed on the land, they'd be in trouble. He gave the order.
"Mister Mathews, bring the ship to a port tack."

All hands were called on deck. The Bo'sun, Mister Mathews, stood along side the Helmsman. He used his Bo'sun's pipe to give the orders to the men at the capstan and the lines. At his order the yard of the fore Mainsail began to swing about slowly, and the Mate said, "Mister Bowman, tell me when she's comin' round."

"Aye, Sir." He pulled the large wheel over to port, and the ship sailed on a bit, then. . . her bow began to move. As he felt the hull beneath his feet, he said, "She's comin' about, Sir."

Again the crew heard the pipe's order and the fore Mainsail yard finished its arc. Following that, the Mainsail yard came next. With the yards braced around and the Jibs shifted, the Spanker swung over to the opposite side of the ship as was expected. Then the crewmen who were not needed, were left to go below.

As the starboard watch went below, John said, "Mister Mathews, your helmsman is tired."

"Aye, Sir. I'm having the helm relieved every two hours, Sir."

"You might want to get two men on the helm during this heavy weather."

"I'll see to it, Sir."

When all was settled, John spoke to William about his speed log. "Mister Becker, is this the only one of these you have?"

"Aye, it is."

"Might I have the ship's carpenter make one for myself?"

"You can. But mind you, these are the latest kind of logs. It could come up missing if another Mate should learn of it. I'd keep a close eye on it were I you."

"I will, and I'll see that yours is returned as soon as mine is finished."

TWELVE ✶

The ship's cook, was clearing away the Captain's breakfast table, when the Captain said to him, "Short Knife, will you ask the Mate to fetch the Pilot and have them join me in my cabin?"

"Aye aye, Sir. I'll see to it, Sir." He left for the cook shack, then passed the word to the Mate.

John had gone to William's cabin and told him the Captain wanted to see them. They both felt they knew what was going to take place, so William gathered his charts for his expectations of the voyage, his Lunar tables, and some sheets of sketching paper.

As they entered the Captain's cabin, Ian greeted them with, "Ah, good. I see you brought along your charts, William. Let's go over them."

"Aye, Sir." He walked to the Captain's table and spread his charts open. The Captain and First Mate joined him. He began with, "For the first leg of our journey on the way to Madeira, if the weather holds good, it could be the easiest part of the trip. A bit more than 1180 nautical miles to the south, then we cross to the West Indies.

This part of the journey is close to, but less than 4000 miles, and home again across the North Atlantic. The voyage will be just short of 7800 miles as the crow flies, and of course we will add some distance to that as we sail."

Ian was working the numbers in his head. "That would be just over two months at five knots and running downwind the entire trip. Wouldn't that be magnificent?"

John smiled at the thought of an easy trip, but said, "We couldn't possibly be that fortunate, Ian."

"Most likely not, John. But not far from it if the weather holds and all goes well." Then he turned to William. "Now tell me about this new trick of yours, the one that saves us so much time."

William smiled. He was pleased to be bringing along the latest theories in navigation. "Well, as you already know, normally a ship's Captain would sail up, or down, to the latitude that would take them to their chosen destination, then sail across that latitude until they reached their port of call."

Both the Mate and the Captain nodded in agreement. Then William continued, "I've a copy of the Lunar tables. It's a published translation of Ptolemy's Geography by Johann Werner. It's a simple method for finding the longitude by using the known speed of the moon and its diameter."

John spoke up, "You mean how fast the moon moves will tell us where we are?"

"It will help us find our position."

William could see the two men were confused, so he continued with a more detailed description. "The distance across the Moon has been discovered, and how fast it moves is also known. The Lunar tables explain the Moon's position at any given hour of any day. So, when you observe the Moon, you measure how long it takes to travel between two known stars. Then you look in the Lunar tables for that time of day, and this helps you fix your position with the longitude."

Ian spoke first, "I'm not familiar with these tables. How will these help us?"

"It means we can sail closer to the true path of our destination. More like the crow flies."

John said, "You're not serious. We can sail diagonally to our destination rather than up or down to a latitude?"

"That is exactly what I mean."

"Is this a proven fact, now?" Ian looked at William for his answer.

"No, it is a recent and new theory, but it seems to work."

"I'm ready to try new things. You just keep us off the rocks."

"Aye, Sir. That is why I'm along on this voyage."

THIRTEEN ✶

They were five days into the trip south, the
weather moderated and the watch had spotted
the coast of Portugal off the port beam late in the
day. It was closer than the Captain and the Pilot,
William, had expected. As the two men stood
near the Helmsman, William asked the
Helmsman, "Does the compass hold a true
course, Jim?"

Jim adjusted the helm slightly as the afternoon
sun began to dip near the horizon. He replied,
"Nay, Sir. It wanders in a rough seaway, Sir."

"Wander? How so?"

William already knew why. Ship's logs in recent
months gave a general indication that the
Captains felt the dry compass card needed to be
dampened. Something to keep the movement
slowed down. A few of the more learned had
suggested that the needle being fastened under
the card made it move awkwardly. It was
commonplace for a Helmsman to steer by a star,
a cloud, or point of land in the distance rather than
trust the compass before him. He himself had
written the Admiralty, as had many other Captains
and Pilots, about this kind of compass. Though
this kind of compass was recommended by the
Naval authorities, he thought them to be poorly
made; they simply did not point true.

He turned his head to listen more closely as Jim spoke. "When the ship heels on a port tack, the compass card swings between South and Southwest, on the starboard tack it swings from South to Southeast."

William watched the compass card for a few moments, then said, "It seems there's also a deviation that I can't account for. I'll check it against my own compass when I go below." As he turned to leave, he continued with, "And I'll start keeping a closer eye on the ship's compass. If you find any other troubles with it, be sure and let me know right away."

"Aye, Sir."

*   *   *

Jack stood at the base of the steps leading into the fo'c'sle. The other hands formed a semicircle around him, listening as he spoke. His hair had gone south long ago, only the hair in his nose and ears had stayed north of his equator. His face was scarred by years of neglect, and of course his right hand with only three fingers drew attention to him.

He looked mean, and he had a bad reputation when he drank too much grog or rum ashore. He explained his curiosity to those close by. "They've locked the hold Mates."

Young Seaman Tom Franklin, who was in awe of Jack, spoke up, "Why do they lock the hold, Jack?"

Jack smiled, a missing tooth showing a gap as he spoke, "I'm not yet knowing that, Lad, but I'll be lookin' to find out."

From the weather deck, they heard as the Bo'sun called below, "All hands on deck!"

Jack spoke quickly, "Mates, I'll pass the word about the hold, soon's I see for me self." The men started topside, the ship was about to tack and the yards had to be braced around and squared to the winds apparent new direction.

While the crew was topside to swing the yards, William passed close by a small group without their notice, and he overheard three of the men talking in hushed tones. Something was being said about the ship's hold.

The words spoken about the hold disappeared from his mind as he entered his cabin to look at his own compass. He knew Jim was steady on the course ordered by the Mate, but his own compass, floating in a closed bowl of spirits, indicated enough difference from the one at the helm, that he knew they would miss Madeira, possibly not even seeing the Island. He'd have a talk with John Davis, the Mate.

FOURTEEN ✷

After William had asked John to his cabin, then showed him his personal compass and explained about the possible compass error of the ships compass, John was concerned. Though he wasn't the ship's Navigator, he didn't want to sail all over an ocean unnecessarily. Midway into Mister Rankin's starboard watch, he decided to check the compass course for himself.

The evening had chilled some, and though they were in the Portuguese trade winds, John pulled a dark, but heavier sweater over his head. Then he started topside. As he climbed the steps to the bridgedeck, he noted something odd about the Helmsman.

It was something he'd seen before with this man at the helm, but at the moment he couldn't place what it was. He'd reached the top step before the Helmsman had seen him coming, and it was the quick movement of the man's hands that caught John's eye. As he closed the distance he said, "How's the helm, Mister Bowman?"

"Steady, Sir." His small beady eyes betrayed a nervousness as the First Mate stood close, even more so when he realized the Mate was looking down at the compass.

As John looked at the hourglass he couldn't believe the time had gone so fast, and then he glanced at the piece of glass covering the lamp compartment to the left. His eyes moved quickly to search the edges of the glass covering the hourglass, to the right of the compass. It too was slightly ajar. Looking into the Helmsman's eyes, he saw a flicker of fear, then the Mate walked forward to the fo'c'sle. He found the Bo'sun, Rankin, sitting at the mess table working on a new sea chest, biding his time on watch away.

The Bo'sun heard him approaching and acknowledged him. "Good evenin' to ya, Mister Davis, Sir."

John got right into the reason he'd come looking for the Bo'sun. "The Helmsman, Mister Bowman, in your charge. Do you know him well, do you?"

"Nay, Sir. This is the first time I've shipped with him."

"He's been warming the glass to make his watches shorter."

"Nay, Sir. You don't mean it?"

"Aye, I do. I saw him move the glass over the lamp as I neared him but a few minutes past. He's to stand extra time on watch to make up for the shortage."

Both men understood the danger of the hourglass being warmed by the lamp at the binnacle. When the glass was warmed by the lighting lamp, the sand flowed quicker and the time on watch would be shortened. It would also change all of the navigation decisions, and could put the ship in grave danger.

The Bo'sun also knew that what the First Mate meant, was that the entire starboard watch section would be standing more time on this watch.

"Aye, Sir. It'll be done, Sir. And the glass, Sir?"

"We're far enough at sea that it will be fine for this night. I'll talk with the Pilot and have him correct it on the morrow."

"Aye, Sir." On the morrow, the Bo'sun knew everyone aboard would know about the glass being warmed. It would not go well for the Helmsman with the crew having to spend more time on watch, and it would not set well with the Captain that the Bo'sun had not caught this man cheating on time before. More than one ship and her crew had been lost at sea because of this simple trick by a watchman.

*   *   *

Jack had been exploring while off watch foregoing some needed rest. He'd known about a loose floorboard plank in the rope locker, when he lifted it he was able to squeeze his body into the opening below, then found his way into the ship's hold by crawling aft through the bilge. In the darkness it smelled rank as some bilge water sloshed around his knees. His feet and hands were often submerged in it as he moved along crawling over ship's ribs and braces. He'd been curious why there was water in the bilge. The ship shouldn't be taking water in these kindly seas.

He'd worked his way around the base of the main mast step, his knees suffering on many of the ship's ribs and the fastenings, but he finally found what he was looking for. A small hatch that opened up from the bilge into the cargo deck above.

This opening was used to allow someone to inspect the bottom of the bilge pump where it sucked water out of the bilge. It was here, in the sump, that someone could clean it if needed. He poked his head up through the hatch to be sure he could gain entry to the hold. He wanted to have a look around, but his time on watch was near, and he dare not miss or be late for watch.

He'd mention it to his mates about the ship having water in the bilge.

FIFTEEN ✶

The Bo'sun, Raymond Rankin, was a short distance behind the Helmsman Bowman as they descended the ladder leading below into the fo'c'sle. Each was tired from an extra long watch, each wanting, and needing rest and to sleep. But, at the bottom of the ladder, they were met by the rest of the starboard watch crew. The look on their faces was not one of forgiveness.

Before the bo'sun's feet even neared the bottom step, someone in the group said to him, "Mister Rankin. I'm thinkin' you're wanted aft, Sir. Somethin' about checkin' the steering cables, Sir."

Bowman was stopped by the group at the bottom of the ladder, but the bo'sun was still on the ladder a step or two behind him. Raymond looked down, his eyes scanning the men below, and he knew they were waiting on his decision to go aft, and he knew he was not wanted here. "Who was it that wanted me to come aft?"

Another voice sounded this time. "Not sure who it was, Sir. Ye may just want to have a look. . . just to be safe, Sir."

He nodded his head yes, but he did not speak further. Then he turned and started back up the wide ladder. He knew there was going to be some trouble, and he knew why. He also knew there wasn't a damn thing he could do about it. Fo'c'sle law was fo'c'sle law. It would be carried out, and the condemned man had to endure whatever was coming his way, if he could.

The Bo'sun stopped just out of view from the men below, but he listened hard. The words were harsh about having to stand an extra long watch. This came about because of Bowman's warming the glass. He also understood that part of the anger was simply because Bowman had gotten caught in the act. None of them would have complained had it gone unnoticed. The older hands also knew such a trick could endanger their lives, and that the ship could flounder on a lee shore.

There wasn't any fist fight. The blows were being landed on one man's body, Bowman's. He did not cry out in pain. He simply put up with the anger being directed toward him. As they beat him he put the names of these men away in his memory. There were two men who did not participate in his pain, Three Finger Jack and Tom Franklin. Jack hadn't involved himself, because he'd been at the mercy of an angry crew before, and Tom stayed out of it because of fear and humiliation of what these men were doing to one of their own.

SIXTEEN ✶

Jose and his brother, Antonio, were speaking with a neighboring vineyard owner, Pinto Fernandez. Antonio's wife, Maria Joaquna, had decided to take her leave of the men but she made sure her words were heard by them as she left. "You should be ashamed of yourselves for what you are doing. God knows it will come back to haunt you."

The men looked at her as she departed the wine cellar. The musky smell of the cool cavern had become second nature to them and they did not notice the odor. Pinto had just brought them news. "Yes, there is another English ship in the bay, but not the same one as before. They want to purchase wines from many of us."

Antonio looked sheepishly, his wife had admonished him after the last ship had left and she had found out what they had done. "You know, we sold bad wines to the last Englishman, and we were fortunate to have gotten rid of a great amount of that last bottling, but it is wrong not to tell these men about the wines."

Pinto defended his actions. "It is not my duty to inform them. They should taste each wine before they make a purchase."

Jose asked, "Does Francisco know about the wines we sold to the last ship's Captain?"

Pinto said, "I did not tell him, and I will not tell him this time either."

Antonio spoke again, "How will you keep it from Francisco this time?"

"I have already arranged a carriage for the ship's Captain. I will see to it that he is driven around the island to each of a few well-chosen vineyards, such as my own and each of yours, if you like, but I will offer my best wines for his tasting pleasure."

"Will you offer some of this last bottling?"

Pinto looked at Jose as he answered, "I may suffer an oversight."

*   *   *

It was a week after the previous ship, the Lady Ann, had gone when Maria met Rosa DeMetrito in the market. She had mentioned the wines and how some had been sold to the last ship from England. Rosa made it a point to tell her husband, Francisco. He would know what to do about the deception, if anything was to be done. He could not prevent the owners from selling wine he thought bad. He could only do the correct thing in his own dealings.

SEVENTEEN ✯

The weather was stable and John stopped at the Captain's door, knocked, and when given permission, entered Ian's quarters. "What is it, John?"

"The crew's still a bit green, Sir. I'd like to practice tacking the ship, Sir."

"An excellent idea, John. By all means do so."

"Aye, Sir."

Arriving at the foreward bridgedeck rail, just in front of the Helmsman, Jim Barnstable, he called out, "Mister Mathews, get Mister Rankin topside and assemble the crew."

He could see men scurrying about putting things in order before going aft to muster. One or two rubbed sleep from their eyes as they came aft. It only took a few minutes before all hands were mustered just below him.

"The weather is perfect for a tacking drill. I'm sure all of you are aware that we lack the proper skills when we have to tack the ship. It does not go smoothly. In fact it is ragged and it is sloppy." He was aware of feet being shuffled about the deck, arms coming up to cross their chests. They knew it was not to be an easy afternoon.

Mister Rankin, Mister Mathews, separate your crews into different sections and we'll get started. Mister Franklin, you'll be taking in the headsail sheets, Short Knife, you're to cast them loose when ordered. Any man not found to be working, will suffer a worse fate."

He looked around, as if he expected questions. Of course none came. "All right then, lets stand by the braces for a port tack."

John turned to Jim Barnstable at the helm, "You ready, Helmsman?"

"Aye, Sir. Ready to tack ship, Sir." Jim planted his feet squarely on the deck, locking his legs in place, his hands on the wheel, arms stiffened for the turning of the large wheel.

"Steer full and by, prepare to come about!" John turned back to the crew and called out, "Hard a lee!"

Jim began to turn the wheel to starboard to bring the ship through the eye of the wind. He did it slow like, so as not to stall the ship, just to keep her turning steadily while the crew worked the yardarms and the sails.

There was silence as the crew waited in their assigned locations, the only noise heard was the creaking of lines pulling taut through the blocks overhead. She started around quickly, but slowed as the wind passed amid ship and past the beam, then worked its way forward to the bow. Just as it was dead ahead, John ordered, "Back your headsails tight to force the bow through the wind's eye!"

Satisfied as the three Jibs started to fill but not yet freed to fly across the foredeck, he continued, "Midship the Spanker." Jim caught sight of the sail over his head swinging to the ship's center, holding there until loosed to fill on the other tack.

As the ship began to swing onto her new course, sheaves rattled in their blocks, and the canvas could be heard as it started flapping. It started high up from the upper topsails first, then down to the lower topsails, and finally the mains. Satisfied, the First Mate called out, "Haul the mains!"

The crew struggled, muscles on arms bulging as hands started clawing at lines to bring her about. Few were working as a team, but working they were. Belaying pins rattled in their sockets like a child's bones in a small coffin, as lines were tied off to keep the sails in trim.

"Loose the headsail sheets." With this command, Short Knife, cast them off starting with the number three Jib, then number two, and finally the number one, each shielded from the changing wind by the sail in front of it. It went smoothly.

"Pass the headsails." Tom Franklin had others to help him pull the Jibs across to the other side of the ship and cleat them off on belaying pins. Number two and three came easily, but when number one passed over the bow, they had to hurry to get it hauled tight and cleated off on a pin. Each would be trimmed proper after the ship had made her turn.

The ship moved through the eye of the wind, and began to settle on her new course. The crew was still pulling the yards into the new position, stronger men moving to the front of the lines to replace those who were unsure.

"Ease the Spanker." The sail over Jim's head began to fill again, its power helping the ship settle, and through the bottom of his feet he could feel her begin to move forward through the sea with more strength.

John's smile could be seen by any who took the time to look aft. He was pleased it had gone as well as it had. "Well done, lads. Now tack her back on her proper course."
He heard a curse or two, but he also knew they expected to return to their original course. It was to the Islands, islands where they could enjoy ladies foreign to them, and as much spirits as each man could afford.

After the ship had settled on her course to Madeira, the Bo'sun, Mister Mathews, spoke quietly to John, "Mister Davis."

John edged closer because of the hushed tone used by his Bo'sun. "Aye."

"I've heard talk between the crew. Seems word has it that we have water in the bilge. The men are concerned, Sir. When I heard about the water I tried the bilge pump, Sir. And surely, Sir, there was water to be pumped. Since then I've pumped it out on the late watch every third day and there never seems to be much to pump. Still, it is there."

"Taste the water, Bo'sun, if you find salt in it let me know, but keep your findings to yourself."

"Aye, Sir." He wondered why the Mate would have him taste the water. If it wasn't salt water, how could it be fresh.

EIGHTEEN ✵

William came topside after the starboard watch had been set and asked the Bo'sun, "Mister Rankin, if you would, Sir, I want to check the compass settings. If I may, I'd like Mister Barnstable on the helm during that time."

The Bo'sun understood this as a request, but a request he'd have to put into motion. "Aye, Sir. The Mate turned, and called out, "Mister Barnstable, to the helm with you."

As Jim hurried aft and settled at the helm, the Bo'sun asked, "Will you be needing the Helmsman, Harmon, Sir?"

"No, but he can stand by to take the helm when I'm done."

"Aye, Sir." This appealed to the Harmon as he would be at rest doing little, if anything, for the time.

"I have a replacement hour glass, Mister Rankin. I'll take the other one to my cabin and correct it later."

"Aye, Sir."

"Mister Barnstable, hold her tight on course whilst I compare the ships compass to my own."

"Aye, Sir."

William opened the lid of a boxed compass. All of the fittings on this box were made of brass and as he held it near the ship's compass, the difference was small but apparent. Even the Bo'sun, who couldn't resist watching said, "Which one is correct, Mister Becker?"

"Mine is the truer course. You can see my compass floats in a liquid, while the ship's compass is dry and has nothing to dampen, or slow the movement." William watched and compared the two compasses a few minutes, then he asked the Bo'sun, "Would you have the ship's carpenter join us?"

"Aye, Sir. The Bo'sun turned to the other Helmsman, Harmon. "Fetch the carpenter."

"Aye, Sir."

In less than three minutes the ship's carpenter arrived on the bridgedeck. "You sent for me, Sir?"

"Aye, but it's the Pilot who wants you."

William pointed to the binnacle, "Can you make me a new binnacle, one without any iron nails? In fact, I'd like one constructed only of wood."

"Aye, Sir. Could take a couple of days or so, Sir"

"Do it then, and when you've finished I want to be here when you mount it to the deck."

William turned to the Bo'sun. "Thank you Mister Rankin. We're through here."

"Aye, Sir. Mister Harmon you'll resume your watch on the helm. Mister Barnstable you can return to your duties."

As both men took over their previous duties, the Bo'sun asked, "Why do you ask for a new binnacle, Mister Becker?"

"Ah, you see Mister Rankin, this one was made using iron nails, and the dry card compass slows as it points to the metal in the woodwork as the needle swings past their location. The new binnacle will be free of iron nails and will read a truer course."

"Am I to understand, Mister Becker, Sir, that we've been following iron nails?"

"That's close to the truth of it, Mister Rankin."

NINETEEN ✳

The Quest raised Funchale, Madeira late in the afternoon and the anchor burrowed into the seabed just as the Sun was setting. The crew was allowed to do as they pleased for the remainder of the day, with the exception of an anchor watch. No one was allowed to go ashore, except the Captain and First Mate and they didn't go until the following morning to clear the ship in through customs. All hands slept soundly that night as the ship lay motionless in the quiet waters of the bay. Only the change of tide could be heard as the small waves rippled against the hull at a different angle. The next morning, after the ship was cleared by customs, the crew moved the ship to the wharf and began making the ship ready for taking cargo aboard.

*   *   *

While the First Mate was over seeing the ship's preparations for cargo, a carriage arrived. It had been arranged by the vineyards on the island that Ian could make stops at each winery. As he toured the different wineries on the lower elevations on the island, he was offered wines to sample. He went to every winery on the lowlands of the island except two.

One belonged to Francisco DeMetrito, his other wineries were in the higher altitudes on the island. The other winery was still selling their wines in casks. It wouldn't be using the newer method of bottling wines until the following season.

An oversight on Ian's part, he never once inquired as to the bottling dates of the wines he was given to sample. In the recesses of his mind he knew that the bottling of wines was a recent discovery. During his tour of the island he arranged for several different wines and, as Richard had requested, payment was to be made in gold when a successful loading had been accomplished.

Not one person, during his touring of the vineyards, had said anything about this year's wine crop, though he had heard someone mention the short and hot season. That person had been quickly given something else to do out of earshot of Ian's touring party.

After the ship had been brought to the wharf, the crew set about opening the hold. They found the three bins, but the third bin was empty and had only a bed of shavings placed inside on the bottom. The owners of the wineries explained they wanted to be sure the loading went well, so they provided a crew to load the cases of wines into the ship's hold.

They started by placing a layer of wine in the third bin first. When the first layer of wine was in place, the ship's crew moved the top layer of wood chips from the second bin, over to the third, using this to cover the first layer of wine cases.

Murmurs ran through the crew as they uncovered large blocks of ice. Both Bo'sun's Mates were working in the hold with the crew, and they themselves had learned what to expect just hours before. Rankin and Mathews started by having the crew move a layer of ice from the number two bin into, and on top of, the wood shavings in the number three bin. Then another layer of shavings was moved to cover the ice, this was followed with more cases of wine. When both bins were fully loaded with wine and ice, they were covered with canvas, and the hold was locked as before.
The Quest's lines were cast off at first light the following morning and the ship's crewmen were not happy. They'd had only one afternoon ashore. As they made ready for sea, no words were spoken between the First Mate and the Helmsman, Bowman, other than the acknowledgment of orders.

John had noticed the blackened eyes when he said, "South by West, Mister Bowman."

"Aye Sir, Sou' by West it is, Sir."

TWENTY ✷

On Monday, Katherine and Margaret were talking as her hair was being done, and Margaret asked Katherine about the man she had seen her wave to on board her husband's ship, the Quest. "You have someone on the Quest, do you?"

"Yes, Mum," she'd answered. "It's Jim Barnstable, Mum. He's a Helmsman and apprenticed to Mister Becker as a ship's Pilot. We're to be wed on his return."

"Katherine, that's wonderful news!" Margaret knew only to well how it was to be a sailor's wife. "I too, was like you, well not quite, but I've spent years alone as my husband sailed the seas. I didn't like it then, and still don't like it. I need my man at home. . . and in my bed at night."

Katherine smiled. She'd caught the meaning of being in bed alone, or thought she had. "Yes'm". . .She thought about it for a few moments before she continued, "I have a woman's toy to help me through some of the nights alone, when I hunger for a man in my bed. I keep it under me pillow. "

*   *   *

Margaret had known Katherine left the house earlier in the morning, and neither of them had planned on Margaret having her hair done today, but an invitation had come to join Elizabeth and

94

other friends during the afternoon hours. Margaret felt certain Katherine would go to her room to put her coat away when she returned, so she had written a note asking to have her hair done on Katherine's return.

She climbed the stairs to Katherine's room, opened her door, and crossed the room to the dressing table. As she placed a note on the top of the dressing table, she remembered what Katherine had said. Curious, she went to the bed and lifted the pillow. It was apparent that one end was indeed a handle. The other end was painted in a light pink color. She was embarrassed as she'd looked, and quickly dropped the pillow. Not bothering to put it back properly, she then left the room.

It was just after nine of the morning when Katherine knocked at her door, and opened it slightly. She poked her head in saying, "You left me a note, Mum. You'd like your hair done. Have I forgotten that you wanted your hair done today?"

"No. No, you didn't but I received an invitation to join Elizabeth and other friends this afternoon, and if you don't mind, my Dear."

"Not at all, Mum. I'll be getting my things then."

After Katherine washed Margaret's hair, she started to dry it, and then rolled it around pieces of cloth she used just for this purpose and to let it finish drying. She used rags for her own. As she worked, she asked. "By chance did you see my toy, Mum?"

Margaret blushed, but she answered, "Yes. I'm sorry. I didn't mean to pry, I just. . . ."

"Oh, I've no problem with you knowing about my toy, Mum, I just wanted to know if it was you or the maid, Jesselyn."

A few quiet moments passed before Margaret spoke, "How does a woman get one of these . . . toys?" The tension of speaking about it passed quickly. Now it was a woman to woman conversation and Margaret just wanted to know more.

"Oh, well you can get one in the women's shop in the square, Mum. You've but to ask Bette quietly, and she will have one for you. She keeps a few for those who need them."

Margaret flushed, as she said, "Oh, I couldn't speak to anyone else about them. I mean . . . . Well, I just couldn't."

If she had looked up into her mirror, she would have seen a smile cross Katherine's face. Again, after a few moments, Katherine said, "What size do you think, Mum?"

"Size! They come in sizes?"

"Oh, yes, Mum. Big ones, little ones, but why anyone would want a little one is beyond me."

They both laughed, but this time their eyes met in the mirror. Margaret said, "One like yours, I'd expect."

After Katherine finished her hair, Margaret dressed, and a hired carriage delivered her to Elizabeth's home where she spent most of the afternoon. On arriving home, she'd gone straight to her bedroom. As she placed her handbag on her dresser, she saw a lavender cloth bag lying on top of her pillow. When she picked it up, she knew immediately what it was. It was a gift from Katherine. She put it back down. *'I'll look at it later.'*

She went to her writing desk, her intention to send a poste to Ian about the new game she'd played at Elizabeth's during the day. They'd had such fun. As she started to write, her eye's darted to her bed and the cloth bag. Again she started to write, but the words would not flow properly. After drawing a line through several of her last words, she stopped. She cleaned the pen, and put the stopper in the bottle of ink. Then she began to undress. *'The poste could wait until the morrow.'*

TWENTY ONE ✷

William expected to sight land sometime the following day. This very morning, at twilight, he'd taken a sight on Mercury to find the ship's position, and notified the Captain that they were closing on their destination. This was good news as they were two days earlier than expected, though Ian was well aware of their position by his own calculations.

Late in the day, just as the Sun closed onto the horizon, the First Mate, John Davis, was standing in the shadows of the Spanker sail and was hidden from view of the main weather deck. He'd heard the boisterous voice coming up from the fo'c'sle. This was just seconds before he heard the splash. It wasn't a loud splash, but the evening was quiet. John noticed the strangeness of it, like a popping sound. Like a sound caused from a cupped, or flat surface. He looked over the side, more out of curiosity than anything else, but what he saw passing by the stern surprised him. He looked quickly forward, but the man had gone back below unseen.

Immediately he went aft and knocked at the Captain's door. When he heard the word, "Come," he went in.

"Captain. Someone is taking wine from the hold, Sir."

Ian was pressed, he hated theft on board his vessels, but it had to be dealt with. "Find out who it is, John."

"Aye, Sir. I'll arrange to watch through the viewing hatches aft. I'll get William to share watches with me."

"Just find the thief, John."

Moments later the Mate knocked on William's door. When it opened, he slid inside. "We've a problem, William. We've a thief stealing wine from the hold."

"And why is that of my concern?"

"It's not your concern, but I'll be needing your help in catching whoever it is in the act. Perhaps you've noticed the small hatch just forward of your door?"

"I have, but I've not thought of it."

"It's for checking the conditions of the hold without going inside. Usually these are used to check on the cargo during heavy storms, but now we'll use it to watch to see who comes into the hold, and how they enter. Come with me and we'll use the one in my cabin. You can start watching now, and we'll change every two hours."

"Why every two hours?" He didn't want to be bothered by this, but John was the ship's First Mate, and what he said carried a lot of influence.

"That'll have us seen more often topside, so's to not alert the crew."

It was just after the morning watch had been spelled at eight bells, that William heard the noise. He reached over to wake John, who had taken a double watch in the early hours. When he shook John's leg, he came awake with a start.

William cupped his hand over the Mate's mouth to still him, then motioned toward the opening. The two men peered inside and waited. Shortly they saw him and, when his hand came up over the top edge of the container, there was no mistaking whom it belonged to. The hand with three fingers pulled back clutching a bottle of wine.

As the Captain was briefed, he had the Mate call the Bo'suns together at the bridge deck. He looked briefly at both men, then said, "Mister Rankin, you've a thief among your watch."

The Bo'sun's head dropped to his chest in disgust, his shoulder's slumped, and he said, "Who be it, Sir?"

"Three Finger Jack."

"His crime, Sir, if I may be so bold, Sir?" He already had his suspicions, he'd noticed Jack smelled of spirits, but couldn't think of how he'd gotten any.

"He's been seen stealing wine from the hold."

"I'm to fetch him, am I Sir?"

"Of course, Man. Bring him aft and muster the crew."

The crew was called aft of the cook shack and Jack was singled out. Reluctantly he came to where the Bo'suns and the Mate stood by the main mast. A Bo'sun now stood on each side, holding him by his arms, as the Captain read the charges against him.

"Know ye, one and all. Three Finger Jack has been seen stealing wine from the cargo hold. He is to be punished for this crime of theft. I can keel haul him, but as you all know, he'd not survive. The barnacles on the bottom of the ship's hull would cut him to shreds or he'd likely drown. I could give him lashes with the cat o' nine tails, but this too, could kill him. Instead, I've decided to test his strength and fortitude. If he can stand at the mast for twenty-four hours, without falling, he will only suffer a cut the ship's sailmaker can sew closed."

Moans from the crew could be heard, each man knew what was coming, as did Jack. Twenty-four hours would seem an eternity.

Finished addressing the crew, the Captain said, "Do you have anything to say, Jack?"

"It's a filthy wine, Sir." It wasn't until later that the Captain understood Jack's meaning.

Jack was pushed against the mast, his face feeling the grain of the wood press into his cheek. His three fingered hand was held against the mast over his head by the First Mate as the Bo'suns held him steady. Then the Mate staked his hand to the mast with a very sharp knife. The knife was pushed through his hand between the tendons of the middle finger and the next one outboard, the ring finger. Then the knife, with the sharp part of the blade on top, was hammered into the mast with a belaying pin.

Jack tried not to admit to the knife as it cut his flesh, though everyone could see he was in pain. Then he was left standing there. Blood started inching down his arm and was dripping onto the deck, but the flow of blood would coagulate and stop before long if Jack didn't fight it. It was to be a long night. As his other arm encircled the mast for support, he could only hope the weather would hold and the ship wouldn't roll in the seaway.

Tom Franklin, the new man aboard, asked the cook, "Short Knife, what'll happen to Jack?"

"If he slips or falls, the knife will cut up through his hand, splitting it wide open."

"Oh my . . ." Tom Franklin turned away from the scene taking place. He almost vomited at the thought.

Short Knife finished with, "A thief will always be punished aboard a ship, Tom. It's the law, and it's in the ship's regulations. Jack knows that."

TWENTY TWO ✳

William spent much of his time instructing Jim
Barnstable on the finer points of navigation and
advanced deep sea piloting. His coastal piloting
skills were already very adequate.
During this voyage they had only the time Jim
wasn't standing watches and that William had free
as well. Today they were going over the course
William had plotted weeks in advance. It was to
take them to the West Indies in as short a time as
possible, if they could follow the courses he'd set
up. The charts were spread on a table in his cabin
and he had laid down the lines and made marks
along the chosen path he wanted the ship to
travel.

"You see Jim, we've been following this route and
the weather has held in the past few days. My
dead reckoning places us here at the time, and
when we get down here . . . we'll sail across the
latitudes to our destination." His fingers indicating
first one location on the chart, then a second
location. "The route I've chosen is South by West
using the Portuguese trade winds, down to
latitude 15* N 00' then south to 13* N 10' and
Bridgetown on the Island of Barbados".

"How close to that course are we sailing?"

"We're very close, most of the time it doesn't vary
more than a degree, and sometimes just a few
minutes away from my dead reckoning position.

Of course, keeping a closer eye on the ship's compass is helping."

"And using your own for comparison helps."

"Considerably."

"Then when you feel a need to change the course, you tell the Mate the new course he's to follow?"

"Most of the time, but usually the Captain and I go over it each evening as well. He's quite good at navigation himself, as I would expect him to be."

"I've noticed that as usual you keep good records of each new sighting you make as well. Will those become available to other pilots for this route after this voyage?"

"They will if Richard Humphry allows."

"Why would he care, you're the Pilot?"

"True, but we are in his employ so the things we learn about this trip and this area, belong to him. He is the one paying for our work, though I'll have my own records to use. You should keep a log book of your findings as well."

"I've been doing this all along. There is so much to learn I cannot keep it all in my head."

"We should be catching the Antilles Current soon now. That should make our daily progress increase. You've the mid watch tonight?"

"Aye."

"We'll use the Astrolabe before you take the helm, and practice taking a sight on the Moon. As you go off watch have someone wake me and we'll take a sight on Mercury before the early morning Sun."

"I want to get a copy of the 'Lunar tables' when we get home. I'm finding your use of them is of great value."

William already had a copy ordered as a gift to Jim, they should be finished by the time they got home. "Don't rush to spend your funds too soon on returning home."

"Nay, I cannot. I'm beholden to Katherine and must take care of those matters first."

"And I shall have a gift for you."

TWENTY THREE ✭

Ian had been up late the night before going over charts with the Pilot. He was still in his night clothes muddling his cabin about when the knock on his door woke him to the ship's needs. Though his thoughts were slightly muddled he gave his standard answer, "Come."

John Davis, the First Mate, stuck his head inside. "You'll want to be seeing this, Captain."

As Ian began to pull on trousers over his night clothes, he asked, "What is it John?"

"Young Franklin's taken it upon himself to be a champion, Sir."

Now Ian was confused. "A champion? How so?"

"It's best you just look, Sir."

When the two men arrived on the main deck, Ian saw what John had meant. Most of the ship's crew also stood watching. Tom Franklin was standing close behind, and supporting the weight of Three Finger Jack. He was doing this so Jack could rest and not fall.

"According to the crew, Sir, he has been there for hours."

Tom was not a strong man, actually thin for a seaman, but he'd fill out after working on ships, if he lived long enough.

The Captain walked slowly to the mast, then he walked around it to survey the situation. "Well, Mister Franklin, you've taken it upon yourself to help Jack out of his problem have you?"

"It's a cruel punishment, Sir." Tom himself was tired, he cared not what others thought. He simply spoke his mind on the matter.

"That it is, Mister Franklin. That it is, but it won't kill him."

"No, Sir, but his hand will never be the same if he falls, sir."

When the Captain spoke again he did it loud enough so everyone could hear him. "Mister Davis join me here at the mast."

The First Mate came to the Captain's side, "Yessir."

"If Mister Franklin fails in his test to be a champion, and Three Finger Jack falls, Mister Franklin is to take his place."

"Aye aye, Sir."

Tom's concern for Jack was replaced with a personal fear. It could become his own hand up there. Still, he could not stop now.

TWENTY FOUR

The weather held fair, and the ship had to tack the yards but three times on the entire passage to Barbados. Each time the crew's ability to handle the ship had improved. John felt confident on his crew's ability to handle the ship in foul weather or fair. It was late in the day when they arrived near the Island and it had been an easy entry into the bay at Bridgetown. The Captain stood at the aft rail while he watched how well the Mate worked with the Bo'suns to bring the ship in quietly to set the anchor in a soft bottom. He felt sure that one day John would become a ship's Captain.

In the early hours of the morning the Captain, accompanied by the First Mate, had gone ashore to clear customs. The Bo'suns had the crew scrubbing the decks clean and attending to rust spots on a few of the ship's metal fittings.

On the way back to the ship after clearing customs, the Captain said, "When we're back aboard, John, ready the Quest to come along side the wharf. If all goes well, we can have our cargo aboard within a few days."

"Aye, Sir, and what of the crew, Sir?"

"They'll be needing some time ashore. Lets keep a short watch set aboard and let the rest go ashore as they please. They'll need to muster each morning, but after the days work they can do as they like."

"That's a kind gesture, Sir."

"Aye, it is. But, they've been at sea for a good while and I've no doubt they'll be feeling a need to spend some time with the local women here. We'll be at sea again shortly, so a bit of a rest ashore will be good for them. You too, can spend some time ashore, John."

"I might do that, Sir. I've to find a gift for my good wife, Rebeka."

*   *   *

It was late the third morning at the wharf, when a man approached the ship's gangway. John saw him coming beforehand and because he was in uniform, he'd sent a man below to call the Captain topside. Both he and the Captain waited to greet the man as he stepped onto the ship's weather deck.

"Morning to you, Sir."

"And to you, Captain."

"We are honored to have you aboard."

He did not respond in a positive manner, instead getting right to the point. "You are short two men from your ship's crew, are you not?"

Ian looked to John, and John did not smile as he spoke. "We are, Sir."

The official asked, "Whom, Sir, are you?"

"The ships First Mate, John Davis, Sir." John could feel the Captain's eyes on him. He'd not yet told him that two men had not returned to the ship for morning muster. Apparently, the man standing before them was someone of authority. Police no doubt.

"Well, Captain and Mister Davis, two of your men are in my prison. They started a fight and caused much damage last night in an Ale House on the public waterfront."

Ian spoke, "We'll send someone around to collect them and to pay the damages. . ."

"I think not, Captain. I will be keeping them for some time."

*   *   *

After he'd left John said, "I'm sorry, Captain. I hadn't been able to tell you sooner about Short Knife and Three Finger Jack not having returned to the ship last night or this morning. I, myself, just learned of this from the Bo'suns."

"This is not good, John. We will likely be sailing two men short."

"Aye, Sir."

TWENTY FIVE

The first seven days in Barbados, the Bo'suns and the crew spent filling the remainder of the ship's hold full of spices. Sweat poured off the men each day as the morning sun rose higher in the sky. The humidity was becoming unbearable. Blocks creaked as nets full of wooden crates and bags of spices came aboard over the side and loaded into the ship's hold. The rest of the hold held the wines in their clay lined containers.

The second week started with the First Mate making the ship ready for sea. After each hard day at work, the crew was given time to go ashore to find what pleasures they might seek. The Captain had given them warning about getting involved with the local women. These were a people who would not tolerate wrong doings to their own kind, though he knew, full well, his warning would fall on deaf ears.

Talk traveled amongst the crew about Three Finger Jack and Short Knife, the cook. All hands had heard about the two of them being imprisoned on the Island. One had been present when the trouble started in the pub ashore. He'd said nothing for fear of being detained himself as a witness, possibly even missing the ship when it left for home.

Someone asked, "Who's to take over the mess with Short knife gone?"

"Have you not found young Franklin missing today? It is he who is to be the new cook." These words were from someone nearby.

"Can he cook?"

"We'll know soon enough."

* * *

William Becker and Jim Barnstable were examining the new binnacle as the last of the ships food stores came aboard. The loading of the spices had been completed just a few hours earlier, and the ship was being readied for sea. Worn lines were freshly tarred, sails checked, jib and mainsail sheets reversed to place the worn ends near the winches or belaying pins.

William and Jim were speaking as they stood at the helm near the binnacle, "Aye, Jim. It will be easier to keep a true course on the trip home with this new arrangement."

"But, William, you're giving up your personal compass."

"Only for a time, and for the good of the ship and a faster and safer passage."

*   *   *

Ian had penned a poste to Margaret two days prior, and it had left on a fast packet ship heading home for England. At the same time, he'd sent Richard a poste about something he'd suspected. It was about the wines they had aboard. His suspicions started when Three Finger Jack had spoken about the *'Filthy Wine.'*

It had been too late to do anything about it, but a few days after the punishment of Three Finger Jack, he'd had John bring him a sampling of wines from the hold. He, John, and William had tasted each, and found the wines were becoming unfit for drinking. The taste was that of bitterness. Each wine they'd sampled suffered some abnormality, from nearly flavorless to that of outright wretched. After they discussed the different tastes, the realization came to them that the wines tasted more like that of vinegar.

Ian knew it was best to inform Richard as soon as possible, and with the packet ship leaving earlier than themselves, it made this news possible. He was dismayed at the possible outcome of such a loss. It would influence the income to 'Humphry Limited', and of course he, too, would suffer a sizeable financial loss as well. The Captain's share would suffer like that of the ship's owner. In this instance, it would also affect his First Mate.

                    *   *   *

The meal served that day, surprised all hands
aboard, including the ship's Captain, the Mate and
the Bo'suns. During the evening meeting in his
cabin, Ian, John and William were about to go
over the ship's planned route home. The topic,
however, turned to Tom Franklin. "The lad can
cook, John."

"Aye, Sir, that he can. I asked where he learned
how to do this. He explained that as a child he'd
spent many hours in his grandmother's kitchen,
and she'd used his helping hands and mind."

"He'd do well as a baker with his own shop
ashore." William voiced this comment without
second thought. He was thinking of the sweet
biscuits he'd been eating.
"You should speak to him about that, William."
And Ian nodded at John's comment.

John continued, "He's been up since four of the
morning. He roasted a pig early enough that the
smells were gone from the ship's kitchen before
the crew woke. He fixed yams and vegetables he
found in the towne square market early this
morning. The corn meal we had in ships stores.
But the sweet biscuits, I have no idea how those
came about."

Ian rose from his chair and went to a cupboard close to his bed. He reached inside and his hand came out with the knife that had been used to stake Three Finger Jack to the mast. The Mate had given it to Ian after he had pulled it out of the mast freeing Jack. Returning to the table he said, "He seems a good lad, John."

"He's been raised proper, Sir."
"Why don't you give him this as a gift of respect? Don't mention our conversation, if you will."

John took the knife, then Ian added, "William, let's have a look at your charts."

TWENTY SIX ✷

Just short of two weeks in the West Indies, the Quest took her leave on the swing of the tide. When the anchor came free of the bottom, she left Bridgetown on an East by Northeast heading in light air. A warm, steamy, overcast sky kept the sun from searing the skin of those on watch as she made her way to sea this first day.

In the early evening William stood by the stern rail taking in the cooling breeze. In his mind he could almost smell the fresh cut hay in the fields around his home as a child. He recalled many parts of his life, even the many months he'd spent at sea with his father, then his eyes caught sight of the Polar star low over the horizon. He steadied his arm by leaning on the rail, then readied his Astrolabe for the navigation fix he needed. When he'd finished with his calculations, he reached over and handed it to Jim Barnstable who had been lost in thought and stood nearby. "Take your sight on the North Star, Jim."

Jim had been looking aft. His mind had been on the beauty of the Southern Cross, the diamond studded night guide they had been using until now. He turned around to face forward, "Aye." His hand reached out to accept the heavy brass instrument. With the ship punching through waves at just about the crucial moment for each sight, it took him three tries before he was satisfied and his findings matched that of William.

The two men then went below to mark their positions on the daily chart for the Captain's review.

The ship's crew was standing loose watches as the ship had been thoroughly cleaned and painted while anchored. They were being allowed to rest except for those doing regular maintenance. A few hands pulled buckets of cool sea water aboard to douse themselves and to wet the deck to keep the seams closed. A few whittled scrimshaw on bones or tusks to sell in the market when they arrived back home. The best sales always happened on the wharf or along the marine bulkhead designed to keep the sea away from the many shops along the waterfront. All went well the next few days, but overcast skies were following them toward the quiet waters just to the north. A few hands felt uneasy, and a few voiced some concern. A few felt it was just a storm brewing, and a few thought it was something else.

Tom Franklin had gained new respect from his shipmates and the Starboard watch Bo'sun, Mister Rankin, had asked the Captain to promote Tom to an 'Able Seaman.' It had been noted in the ship's log. But rumor had it that Tom had had a talk with the Mate, and John Davis had suggested that Tom should consider opening a bakery on the wharf when they returned home.

However, it took coins of the realm to fill these kinds of wishes, and most seamen saved just enough to last them until they signed aboard the next ship.

Every man in the fo'c'sle had noticed the knife in the leather sheath now shoved in Tom's waist band. Every one of them knew that this was the knife used to punish Three Finger Jack and taken from the mainmast. They also knew the First Mate had given it to Tom, and First Mates on ships were not known for being impressed.

TWENTY SEVEN ✲

This, their fourth day at sea, was overcast with occasional patches of fog, and it was a fog that killed sound before it could travel from one end of the ship to the other. A blanket of mist that hung heavy in the air brought with it a chill and a dampness that made its way through most clothing.

The port watch Bo'sun, Mister Mathews, stood at the Helmsman's left shoulder and was looking to Starboard as the two spoke about the lack of a proper sailing wind. Suddenly, he felt a chill sweep through him, like none he'd ever experienced before. When it penetrated him, he glanced up into the eyes of Mister Bowman standing at the helm. There he saw a change come over the man's face. The eyes he looked into were showing a fear as if God, himself, was issuing a threat to the man's well being.

Just as suddenly Mister Bowman raised his arm and gestured beyond the Bo'sun's shoulder. As Daniel Mathews started to turn, his eyes raked the ship's weather deck below. He saw Seaman Samuel hiding behind the bulk of the main mast, oddly peeking around the curvature of the wood to see what lie beyond the port rail. Then, further forward his eyes caught another man hiding behind the foremast. Still further forward, two men were crouching behind the capstan.

A quick glimpse told him others had just dropped down the fore hatch into the fo'c'sle as if to escape the open deck.

As he finished his turn around, his eyes took in the dark lines of a ship nearly without color, a ship looming even larger than the one on which he stood. Well weathered she was, silver gray with age, drooping sails showing their wear over the years. A few were tattered. Even then she sailed a bit faster through the quiet sea than the Quest, no matter the lack of a breeze in the open sea. She made no wake in the surface. The water gave no notice of her having been there.

His eyes searched the ship's deck for signs of life. None was seen until he looked aft to the raised bridgedeck. There he saw a man in a full length black coat, hair of silver, with a tall hat crowning his head. His mouth opened as if to speak, but Mathews heard no words come forth, he only saw the man's arm come up, as if to beckon them. Then at the last moment he thought he might have seen eyes looking out from the large windows on the aft cabin. He didn't notice faces, just the haunted eyes.

Mathews spoke just loud enough to be heard, "Seaman Samuel."

Samuel, startled, looked aft to the bridgedeck. "Aye, Sir."

"Be quick about it, go below and fetch the First Mate topside."

Samuel jumped from his perch behind the mast, and quickly disappeared aft, fear helping him on his way.

*   *   *

John Davis woke to someone's hand as it shook his ankle. "What? Who is it?"

"Mister Davis, Sir. It's I ,Sir. Seaman Samuels, Sir."

"What is it lad?"

"The Bo'sun sent me, Sir. You'll be wantin' to see this, Sir. It's a ghost ship, Sir."

"Nay lad. . . ." But he could see concern on the man's face, "A ghost ship, you say?"

"Aye, Sir. We'n seen her, she's just off our beam, Sir, passing like a whisper and like the quiet in the grave yard. Spooky like she is."

"I'll be right along."

"Aye, Sir. . . Should I fetch the Captain topside, Sir?"

"Let him be. He's not felt well as of late."

"Aye, Sir." And he was gone.

John had not undressed. Tired, he'd taken his boots off only hours before. He'd stood a long watch earlier when the wind had gone abaft the port quarter, then stopped altogether. He and William had placed the ship's original compass at the base of the new binnacle.

They were experimenting during the lull in weather to adjust this compass by placing small lode stones in various places around it. Neither really trusted the original ship's compass, though it had seemed to be more reliable since it had been removed from the old binnacle built with iron nails and placed in a housing made entirely of wood.

As he moved out of his cabin to make his way topside, he noted his ship, the Quest, made little movement. It seemed she was dead in the water, still and quiet like.

When he came out onto the open deck, he could feel the thick fog surrounding the ship and the damp blanket began to seep into him. He couldn't see more than a few feet past the rail, and he couldn't see his own ship's bowsprit because of its being hidden in the grey shroud. He looked up to see the Bo'sun's Mate near the helm. Arriving on the bridgedeck, he asked, "And, Mister Mathews, where be this ghost ship of yours?"

"She's there, Sir. " His hand pointed off the port beam. The Bo'sun was clearly nervous, as now there was nothing to be seen where he pointed. "She was there, Sir. Me self and the crew saw her just there, Sir."

The Helmsman, Bowman, spoke up. "Aye, Sir. She passed us close by, she did. The fog cleared some, and she comed out of the fog, she did."

"How is it she's sailing in still air, and we are not, Mister Bowman?"

" I dun'no that, Sir, but she did, Sir."

"Did you get her name as she passed by?"

The Bo'sun spoke, "Nay, Sir, just as she passed us close by, she changed her course, she did, turned her stern to us like a woman's rump, Sir. Then she turned off and the fog swallowed her up before we could see the name on her stern, eerie like it was."

"Did you see anyone topside?" John asked the Bosun.

"None, 'cept one. I'm thinkin' it be her Captain. He stood on the bridgedeck beckoning us, but no sound came from his mouth, only an arm waving us to follow along with him." He thought about telling about the eyes, then changed his mind.

"You say there was a man topside aft?"

The Bo'sun answered, "Aye, Sir."

"And would he wearing a top hat?"

Both the Bo'sun and the Helmsman looked at John. They had seen the man aft on the bridgedeck, and they had seen his hat, but it was Mister Mathews who asked, "You know of this ship, Sir?"

"Nay, I do not, only of her legend."

"Thankin' the Lord we didn't follow her, Sir," the helmsman said, a shiver of fear sent his body in a tremble.

John looked his way, "Why do you say that, Mister Bowman?"

"The edge of the world is out there, Sir."

TWENTY EIGHT ✷

On the seventh day at sea, the Quest had been making five knots through choppy seas. Suddenly she shuddered almost to a dead stop. All hands were knocked about the decks. One man aloft had been thrown off the yard on which he'd stood. Had it not been for the ratlines, he'd have fallen to the deck, and possibly been killed. The sails, still full of air, tried to move the ship ahead and she did so, but with labor. As the crew came back to their senses, most were soon on deck to see what had happened. The Captain, the Mate and William joined the others on the weather deck. All hands moved forward to the bow to see what had caused the problem.

The sight filling the eyes of all who looked over the side, was a vision of the sea at the bow awash with blood. The Quest had struck a whale. It had not been killed in the impact, but badly wounded. John barked an order to haul the sails to spill the wind, and to ease the ships way through the water. Then he had two men go below to check the bilges for leaks. A quick search revealed that none had been found.

The hull had withstood the impact without damage. The injured whale, thrashing wildly, freed itself from the stem timber and swam awkwardly away.

Two men had cracked ribs, one a cracked arm, but within a week the pain from their wounds had dropped to a dull ache. As a result of its wounds, the whale died three days later.

The heat at the equator turned intense as the ship wallowed in the doldrums. A man was aloft at the masthead, scanning the sea all around. His purpose, just to look for a freshening breeze of any kind. The men who stayed topside, took turns hoisting buckets of water aboard to pour over one another to cool off. The water made its way across the deck, through the scuppers and back to sea. The deck planks steamed as they dried anew. The seams kept wet also kept the planks swelled. A few men hid under canvas tarps rigged for just the purpose of providing shade.

It was two nights later that a faint stirring was felt in the air, and all canvas was hoisted to escape to the north. By daybreak, it was apparent the weather was going from being becalmed to more wind than they might want.

TWENTY NINE

It was late in the day, just after four bells, when a fast moving low pressure area caught the ship and the skies darkened quickly. Jim was on the helm for the first time in a blow since leaving home waters, though it was not an uncomfortable situation to him. As the storm began to build, he tightened his grip on the wheel and spread his feet farther apart. He did it for better control of the helm and to help him maintain his own balance.

He always marveled at how large the ship was while tied to a wharf, and how small she was in heavy weather as storm swells rolled under her keel. As she rolled on through the night, she continuously pitched her bow through the oncoming onslaught, as if to test King Neptune's rule. She would shudder as each big wave came aboard over the bow, washed down the length of the weather deck, then overboard through the ample scuppers. The sky, black except for an occasional star seen through a rip in the clouds, scudded overhead.

Bo'sun Rankin, seeing Jim's struggle as the seas grew, called out over the wind,
"Mister Franklin, lay aft to give a hand on the helm."

Jim watched as Tom struggled aft, holding onto anything that would take his hand. When he stood at Jim's side, Jim said, "Hold her firm, plant your feet square on the deck and get the feel of her. You'll learn soon enough."

As Tom gripped the wheel, Jim let go, saying, "I want you to know how she feels without my help, then I'll join you again."

"Aye, Jim."

Jim had been aware of rogue waves coming on them about every quarter hour, so he was ready to lend a hand, but he didn't mention that condition to his helper. " A touch to starboard, just a few spokes. . . Now ease her back."

Tom laughed. This being his first time at the helm, he said, "Aye, Jim. This is glorious!"

Jim knew he was feeling the power of the ship through the bottom of his feet and the tug on his arms as he held the wheel. The ship was standing tall and strong to the wind, her square sails dampening the pitch and yaw, then the rogue wave came. Jim had just put his hand on the wheel when she was struck. Tossed on her beams ends, her masts swung like branches of a tree. Then she struggled to right herself and to carry on once again. When their eyes met, on the ship's recovery, Jim saw, not fear, but awe in the eyes of Tom.

"How can anyone in the fo'c'sle sleep through this, Jim?"

"Not many will. It is worse up there than in a debtors prison." He remembered his own past experiences in storms, his arms and legs bracing against the sides of his bunk.
He would sleep a fitful sleep, often more tired after trying to rest, than as if he'd stood a full watch topside facing the weather.

The storm blew a real howler of forty knots the next two days. The waves were big, about twenty five to thirty five feet, and this measured from the bottom of a trough to the top of the next wave. While full of air, a fore royal spar snapped, it's stretched manila sheet parted with the sound of a rifle shot. Several hands raced up the shrouds and ratlines to secure it.

The natural instinct for survival against the sea commanded the action even before the Bosun had a chance to give the order. The ends of the spar were pulled in close and the sail bunted up and pulled close to the broken yard. It was much too dangerous to lower it to the deck at the time. It would have to wait. Being a smaller spar, they did have a spare lashed down on the weather deck, but it could not be replaced until quieter weather.

Other than the broken spar, the ship suffered only minor damage, one rip in the outer jib, which would soon be sewn closed after it was dropped to the foredeck.

The horizon was lost to the eye, only the cutting tops of waves were to be found. No one spoke. A gale, as does the doldrums, induces silence. The fo'c'sle had the smell of bittersweet vomit. Even a few of the more hardy hands were succumbing to the rages of the storm. Breathing the air trapped forward, left each man feeling a dense fog in his brain, those sick were sure they had a dead animal in their gut.

THIRTY ✶

Reginald Bowers, a trade competitor and a friend, was sitting across from Richard in his office. As he was soon to learn, the hour was dark for his friend. Richard had asked his secretary, Martin, to fetch some cold water for Reginald to drink as they spoke.

"Richard, I'm ruined! Ruined I tell you! All of the wines I just received on my ship, the Lady Ann, were filthy. The taste is simply ghastly! No one would ever purchase wines this bad." His head dropped to rest in his hands. His elbows were resting on his knees. Richard heard a gasp of despair escape Reginald's lips.

Richard was concerned for his friend and for himself. "Where did your wines come from?"

"The Lady Ann is just back from Madeira, of course."

Before continuing, Richard sat down, his mind racing at the news that could affect him as well. "Reginald, surely you can recover."

"Nay, I think not. I have immediate orders to fill. Promises I've made. I'm ruined!"

"What will you do with the wines?"

"I've already given the order to dispose of them, to pour the contents down the sewer. They will be gone on my return."

The two men spoke a few more moments as Richard tried to sooth his friend's feelings of despair, then Reginald took his leave. After he'd left the offices of Humphry Limited, Richard called Martin back into his office. "Martin, I have need for several letters to be written, and for you to deliver them in the next few days."

"As you wish, Mister Humphry. What would you have me say in the letters?"

"We'll go over that first thing in the morning, but be sure you use our best company paper. It has to be impressive. We've to sell a product we don't normally have in our stores."

After Martin left, Richard opened the poste he'd received just the day before. This was the second time he'd read it this morning. It did not spell out the problem that Ian had found with the wines in the ship's hold, but now he felt sure he knew what to expect. He had to act fast, or he too would suffer badly.

He wanted to avoid a similar fate of that of his friend Reginald. Richard began to make plans just in case his wines were found to be in the same state.

His sale was to be of the finest vinegars found in the world. No self respecting cook could do without these new vinegar vintages that Humphry Limited just discovered.

THIRTY ONE ✷

The sun had passed its meridian some five hours before and now, as the onshore breezes began to die, the ships timing as it entered the bay had been perfect. With his head cocked, Ian looked forward at the Jibs, then closer to check on the Spanker, his mind weighing the affect on the ships progress. They lay still and quiet. His eyes dropped from the canvas to gauge the distance to the wharf as the ship ghosted in very close. Satisfied, he said,

"Drop your canvas, Mister Davis, then lay us along side the wharf."

John, himself watching the ships progress, knew that Captain Hawkins was a master of sailing a ship right up to a wharf. For that matter the whole towne of Still Water knew it and often watched as the Quest came home. First Mate John followed the Captain's instructions. "Mister Rankin, get your canvas down and standby to lay along side the wharf."

"Aye, Sir." The Bosun gave his orders and the Spanker sail, and the flying and outer Jibs were dropped. Then the ship's crew, fore and aft, readied the ships mooring lines soon to be passed to those on the Humphry Ltd. wharf as needed.

The Mainsail, Fore Mainsail and the Topsails were taken in when the ship was well inside the bay leaving her Jibs and Spanker to drive her the remainder of the distance.

Everyone watched the ships progress as it neared the wharf, especially those on the wharf. There were wives, sweethearts, the warehousemen who would begin unloading the cargo, and Mister Humphry. John waited until he felt she would end her voyage well, then he said, "Mister Barnstable, put your helm hard to port. Lay the stern to the wharf."

"Aye, Sir. Hard a port, Sir." Jim began to turn the big wheel slowly at first so as not to stall the ship on her path. Then, as she neared the wharf, he swung it over faster. Then he waited until he felt the ship nudge the timbers on the wharf. As the lines went over the bow and stern, the ship was lashed to the huge bollards securing her fast. Then Jim spun the wheel back until the rudder was amidship. To finish the voyage he lashed a spoke on each side to keep it in place.

"Mister Davis."

"Aye, Sir."

"I'm going below. When Mister Humphry comes aboard, will you show him to my cabin?"

"Aye, Sir. . . .And your good wife, Sir?"

"She'll be impatient, but ask her to wait until I've had a chance to speak with Mister Humphry."

The Bosuns had not waited for their next orders. They just started the preparations.
A mainmast yard was swung out, a block and tackle swinging loose was dropped and a seaman shackled it to the waiting gangway ashore. One end was lifted by the end of the yard, and fastened to the ship's weather deck at the gate in the rail. Once it was secured, the block and tackle was removed and the ship's business began. Margaret held back so the onrush of others wouldn't rumple her new dress, but the ship's owner, Richard Humphry did not hold back. He charged fully ahead. At the top of the gangway he was met by the ship's First Mate. "Mister Humphry, Sir. The Captain asked me to escort you to his quarters, Sir."

"Very well, John. A good voyage was it?"

"Nearly so, Sir. A few events you'll find in the ship's log." When they were aft, John knocked at the Captain's door. He opened it slightly saying, "Mister Humphry's here, Sir"

Ian had just finished changing into fresh clothing as the knock came at his door. "Bring him in, John."
John stood aside, announced, "Mister Humphry," and Richard entered the Captain's cabin. It smelled of many days of being closed up at sea.

139

The scent of clothing that needed to be laundered was also in the air. It would take some airing to freshen the room.

As John started to close the door behind him, he heard, "John, would you have Mister Franklin bring us some tea and some of those sweet biscuits he makes."

"Aye, Sir."

*   *   *

By the time Tom Franklin had finished pouring tea for the two men, Richard had already eaten two of the sweet biscuits. "These are quite good. . . . Mister Franklin, is it?"

"Aye, Sir, and yes, Sir, Franklin, Sir."

Ian spoke up before the conversation turned to ships' business, "Young Tom wants to open a bake shop in towne."

"Ah, do you now?" It was unusual for a seaman to have a real direction in life and it interested Richard.

Tom was embarrassed, but he answered, "Aye, Sir, but I've to find the monies for it, Sir."

"Ah, yes. . . . Well, you should do well."
When their brief conversation had ended, Ian spoke again, "Mister Franklin, will you ask the Mate to bring Missus Hawkins aft to join us in a few minutes?"

Just as Tom was about to leave the Captain's cabin, Richard spoke to him again.
"Mister Franklin."

Tom turned on his heels, "Aye, Sir."

"If, you've the time, will you stop by my office in the next few days?"

"Yes, Sir. Of course, Sir." His head began to swim. He dared not think of the possibilities that could lie ahead with a conversation with such a powerful man as Mister Humphry. He was ecstatic with the invitation.

THIRTY TWO

The first two days were spent unloading the wines. The spices were to follow. The wines were taken to a Humphry warehouse, cleaned, and new labels put on each bottle. There were several different varieties, but in essence the labels were similar.

'Humphry's Fine Vinegar Imports.' The smaller print indicated that only the finest patrons would be using these for their meals. The sales of this unusual vinegar started with enthusiasm, and the sales were brisk and rewarding to the company. Following the intensity of the sale Richard was quick to get a poste off to the vineyards in Madeira.

The poste went to Francisco DeMetrito. As he was the spokesman for the wineries, all correspondence went through him. Though he knew, now, what had taken place, he passed the word around to each owner, whether he approved of their business standards or not. Every winery on the island was quick to respond to this request.

They were happy to have someone offer to purchase every bottle of this year's wine, though they wouldn't be loaded as cargo until the next season. They all knew of the wines condition and they knew the wines were terrible.

The offer that came from the English buyer would only be enough money to cover the cost of the bottles with little more, but the season would not be a complete loss.

On the first day of unloading the cargo of spices, John saw a familiar face in the work force on the wharf. As the man started to walk up the gangway for another sack, John started down. The man stopped at the bottom to allow John passage. As their eyes met, John said, "And your health, Sir?"

He smiled, "My health be good, Sir, and I'm warm, Sir."

They both saw the humor in this, as the waters of the bay were very cold in the spring when John had thrown him over the side. John continued, "If you've a mind, I can see to it that your name is placed on a list as a welcome crewman aboard a Humphry ship."

"That'd be most welcome, Sir."

John offered his hand and it was taken. "Good day to you, Mister Rawlins."

"Good day to you, Sir."

THIRTY THREE ✮

Richard had offered Tom Franklin some monies to get started and, more importantly, had offered a shop for his use. As he surveyed the shop area he found it was little more than a doorway with a window to the left side, but it was long enough to have his shop in the front and a cookstove just beyond that. The next room could be his larder, and the last room would be his quarters.

His mornings started at the early hour of four, and he worked continuously until nightfall. At the end of his average seventeen-hour days he was exhausted. He began with his goods on display on a table he'd made from wood planks gotten in trade from the ship repair yard. The hastily built tables were covered with worn, but clean, sailcloth.

On occasion he had some small items left, and he began to give broken sweet biscuits to the children of the area. These small gifts resulted in his good fortune, as it was but a short time until their mothers were making purchases. In the beginning he only sold his sweet biscuits, sweet breads, and hard rolls. This changed rapidly as he began to experiment with things his grandmother had taught him. He produced a few pies, which barely had time to cool before they left his shop.

In a short time he'd repaid Mister Humphry the monies owed him. Now it was only a monthly fee for the shop.

One day, as he struggled to stay awake between customers, a young woman came into his shop. He rose from the bench where he'd been resting, wiped his hands on his apron, and approached her. He'd not seen her in his shop before and he said, "Good day, Miss. Would you like a sample of my fresh bread?"

"I would like a sample, but I've not a penny to spend. . . . I've need of a position, Sir." Her hair, coal black, was in a long braid and plunged nearly to her waist. A cap held the loose strands in place, her dress was modest, but filled well. Her eyes were a cool, deep blue. They had a depth he'd not seen before, as if she could see beyond him.

He'd given her an ample sample of bread, then stood looking at her. In his eyes she was marvelous but no words he was comfortable with came to his lips. No one had ever asked to be employed by him before. He was working hard, and knew he could use the help. She waited for some kind of reply. He had to say something! "We start at four of the morning."

He saw a smile widen her face in a pleasing manner that warmed him. "I can be here on time, Sir."

"Starting on the morrow?"

"So be it, Sir."

As she left the shop, he saw her skipping up the walk. He liked her, but he'd not gotten her name. Already she was causing some desire in him.

He'd started a fire in his stove a short time before, but now when he entered his shop from the back, just before four of the next morning, he saw her waiting outside the door. He rushed to let her in. "You're chilled! Come by the stove."

As she rubbed the heat into her flesh from the new fire, he asked, "How long have you been here?"

"I don't know, but I didn't want to be late, Sir."

"I'd rather you were late than frozen. Don't be so early on the cold days."

She smiled at his concern for her well being. "Very well. Late, rather than too early."

"You've a name?"

"Lissa. And you, Sir."

"Tom Franklin, and Lissa . . .please do not call me, Sir."

By the time the shop was opened for the day's business, Tom had explained how he had been doing things. He also explained how he'd been experimenting with different cakes and pastries. She mentioned a few things that her own grandmother used to make, but that she herself made them differently than most others. This first discussion began to have an effect each day, as the two of them brought some interesting pastries to the counter for sale, and none went to waste.

Within months the two were wed, and shortly thereafter found moving into a larger shop. They had had to hire two other young women as employees and were thinking of adding one more. Business was doing very well and Lissa, not a shy woman, had the occasion to speak with Mister Humphry. This came about when she'd taken him some sample of new breads now being made in their shop. He'd been impressed with her proposal and accepted a contract with the two of them. They were now to supply Humphry Limited with breads, biscuits and hardtack for the beginning of each voyage.

THIRTY FOUR

It had been weeks since John had seen Captain Hawkins, though he knew that the Captain and Richard Humphry were in constant touch with one another. They often shared their personal views on differing subjects, most of which surrounded the business and the running of the company ships. He, himself, had shipped on five of the seven ships in the fleet, each one larger than the last. He had shipped with Ian Hawkins as Captain, and the good Captain had been constantly moving up in the chain of command. He now had a great deal of influence, not only in business circles, but in the community as well.

This November seemed warmer to most of the townspeople. Even he and Rebeka had given up wearing their heavier clothing. They were also aware that the real winter months lie ahead of them. Still, it could be a warmer winter than usual. As John entered the office of Richard Humphry, Martin rose from the oak chair at his raised podium. "Mister Davis. They be waiting on your arrival, Sir."

"They? Who are 'they', Martin?"

"Captain Hawkins and, of course, Mister Humphry, Sir."

"Any knowledge of what this be about?"

"I'm sorry. I'm not privileged with that knowledge, Sir."

John was certain he was privileged but couldn't, or wouldn't, say. Martin led him to Richard's private door and opened it saying, "Mister Davis has arrived, Sir."

As John entered the room, both men rose to greet him. "John, Please, join us. Would you join us in a libation."

John was surprised. He tried to act normal, but he'd never been treated in this manner in this, or any office before. "Yes, Sir, I will, Sir."

Richard said, "John, sit there . . . if you will. I'll get you a rum or a sherry, if you like."

John sat in the chair closest to Richard's rich red mahogany desk, as had been pointed out. To be served something in this lavish office was a treat. He took a chance. "I'll try that sherry." He always thought of sherry as a gentleman's drink.

His drink came in an ample silver cup. Then Richard said, "John, Ian and I have been going over our shipping plans for the new year. Though we haven't discussed this with you until now, we felt it is time for your input." He continued without waiting for a response from either of them.

"You see, I've committed monies to purchase all of last years wines from every winery on Madeira."

Ian interrupted. "As you already know, John, though the wines we brought home were all bad we, yourself included, did well with their being sold as fine vinegars."

"Aye, Sir. And I'm grateful for that, Sir."

Richard continued, "Well, John, we have to go back for the rest of the wines this next season."

He'd expected part of the Humphry fleet to set sail before long. "What ship do we sail in, Sir?"

John saw both men smile, and a glance passed between them as Richard said, "Two ships are to make the voyage. Ian will take the Quest, like this past voyage, and the Celeste will accompany her. She's on the hard at the time, but her repairs and refitting are complete. Of course, you'll be on the Celeste, and we need your recommendations as to the selection of crews."

John had been asked for his choice in crewmen on past voyages, but something had been left out of this part of the conversation. He had to ask, "Who's to captain the Celeste, Sir?"

"Why, John Davis, you are to be her Captain. You've served this company well for years and we felt it is time for you to command a ship of your own."

*   *   *

John walked home in a daze. He still could not believe what had just happened to him. *'A ships Captain, a ships Captain.'* The implications were staggering. A position of prestige, a larger share of the profits, more responsibility, and more sleepless nights. He was also aware that his relationship with the men aboard would change. Now he would make the choice when it came to punishment as needed. This he did not relish.

When John entered the warmth of his cottage, Rebeka was feeding the children, and she would see to his meal now. He sat at the table, but said nothing as he watched the children. Rebeka rose to fix him a midday meal, and noted he was quiet,

"What is it, John?"

"I'm to sail on the Celeste in the spring. We've a voyage to Madeira planned."

"Well, John, we both knew you would be going back to sea."

"But, Becky, I'll no longer be serving as First Mate on the ship."

She stopped with his plate only partly filled with his meal. This comment caught her off guard. "What's happened, John?"

"I've a new position to fulfill."

She came to his side, her hands drying on a cloth as she neared him. The plate was left behind, forgotten for the moment. "What position would that be?"

"I'm to be her Captain."

THIRTY FIVE

John had spent nearly every waking hour aboard the Celeste getting her readied for sea. He'd selected Mister Daniel Mathews as his First Mate. John had found him to be an excellent Bosun and a man he wanted aboard on his first ship and in a position of control. Daniel was known around the docks as an artist. His scrimshaw carvings sold quickly and for high prices. Even then it was resold in many instances, to those who collected the finer work.

He too, was having a hard time adjusting to his new position on board a ship. He was no longer someone who just took orders, he gave them as well. Having started as an able-bodied seaman, he'd worked hard on each ship he'd served on and now found himself as a First Mate on the good ship Celeste. John Davis had seen to his promotion and he would do the best he possibly could for Captain Davis. He knew that only good could come from his association with this new Captain of Humphry Limited, but now he himself would be in position to make decisions that affected many others. He felt that if he needed help in making a decision, he had only to ask John Davis.

Rebeka and the children too, had spent many hours aboard. She was putting a woman's touches into her husband's quarters. A quilt she'd just finished after two years work adorned his bed, and one other blanket she had personally purchased with great care. This world of being a ship Captain's wife was bringing some unique changes into her life. She liked this new role.

Margaret and Ian had invited the two of them to their home for an afternoon tea, and Margaret told her, "Rebeka, come see me on the morrow. We will start preparing you to entertain the ladies of our group." Within days Margaret had introduced her to other influential women in towne, women who were wives of ships Captains, or in the shipping business in some manner. The upper crust of society, at least on their level. With Margaret's influence, there was no one to question Rebeka's position among the ranks.

She stopped to rest as she put John's cabin in order, there were some things weighing heavy on her mind. She was trying to decide what to do when John came into his cabin to find her sitting on the edge of his bed. The children were fast asleep behind her, snuggled into their father's quilt.

He'd caught her in deep thought when he entered, and he looked into her dark eyes, "What is it Becky?"

"I don't know what to do, John."

He knew this was not a usual matter she was concerned about, this seemed deeper. He moved close to her, leaned over putting his face close to hers and their lips met. Then he backed off slightly, "To do about what, love?"

"John, Margaret has been introducing me into our new circle of friends, but I've not the proper clothing, nor the education, for finery."

He smiled, "I too, am finding it difficult to change to this new world of ours. Does it seem as if Margaret is really trying to help you learn, or is she just being polite?"

"Oh, no, John. She's quite serious."

"Then, I'd say you should make yourself as available as you can. Seek her advice on attire, then see to getting it. Anyone who has a problem with payment or a line of credit, can inquire of Martin at Humphry Limited. "

"What can Martin do?"

He felt she had ample funds because of his share from the latest voyage, still he said, "He will see that your financial well being is established, and there will be no further questions."

She smiled, put her arms around his neck and their lips met again. "Thank you, John. Will you bring the children home when you've finished for the day?"

"Of course, My Love. Where are you off to?"

"I'm to see Margaret to get the name of the shops that are best for my new clothing. The social manners will come to me as we go along."

He bowed to her as if she were royalty. "My Love, the children and I will see you at the cottage later in the day."

"Yes, and, John, we need to talk about our cottage." She still seemed as if in a serious mind set as she took her leave.

After Rebeka left, his mind searched for an answer to what her last words meant.
'What about our cottage?'

Jim finished stowing his gear in the Pilots quarters just forward of the Captains cabin. The Astrolabe, his most important navigational tool, was cradled in a fine cloth. New to him, but not its use, it would help him read the height of the Pole Star on its scale. With that information he could find the latitude of his ship.

He knew that John Davis, his Captain, understood how to navigate, but Richard Humphry had hired him as a Pilot for this coming voyage. Mister Humphry had explained to him that he was considering using Pilots on each of his ships in the future. Jim reasoned that the cost to Humphry Limited would be huge if he had to purchase all of the latest navigational tools that were being found. Then, each captain would have to be schooled in their use. It would be better for the company to keep Pilots employed who had the latest tools instead. Jim felt sure that if this trip went well, he would have steady employment with Humphry Limited Shipping.

When he'd received the news about his new position two months ago, he and Katherine were wed. Now, here he was making preparations to leave her while he went to sea once again. Though they had wed, Katherine still looked after Margaret's tresses, but now it was more as a friend and confidant.

She still earned a handsome wage from Margaret, but the two of them spent many hours just chatting as well.

As he contemplated his surroundings in the Pilot's cabin, he picked up the replica of William's speed log. He fingered it briefly, then his fingers lifted the recent poste from the top of his small chart table and he read it again.

'My dear friend, Jim Barnstable. Luck has seen fit to send me to sea on the good ship Aries. She is a smaller ship than I've become accustomed to, but we are outward bound to the west in exploration. I expect to return with charts of unknown areas never before seen or recorded. I will try to find you upon my return so that we may exchange news on some exciting lands well beyond our present horizons. I've been thinking of a new venture in the world of Navigation. We'll speak of it on my return.
Your friend, William Becker'

As he put the poste down, he laid it on top of his recent copy of Johann Werner's book on Lunar tables, a published translation of Ptolemy's Geography. He marveled at such a simple method for finding the longitude by using the known speed of the moon and its diameter. This book too had been a gift from William before he took his leave, and he had given Jim the name of a local watchmaker he'd found quite inventive. He visited the watchmaker just recently, and while there he made a purchase. He'd found a new compass that he thought to be even better than William's.

A knock on his door brought him around to the present. At the the door when he swung it open he saw Mister Mathews, the First Mate, and he said, "Your lady awaits you on the wharf, Pilot."

"Thank you, Mister Mathews. I shall join her ashore."

As Jim walked down the gangplank, Katherine joined him, smiling she placed her arm in his as they started walking toward their meager peasants lodging, just a few streets away from the harbour. She walked in silence for a few minutes, then said, "Jim, should we be thinking of finding a cottage of our own?"

This thought had been crowding his mind too. "Yes I think we should. As a Pilot my wage will be enough to provide us with something other than a room, and we've paid our landlord long enough."

"I've a stew hot in the pot, Dear Husband." She reached up with her other hand and squeezed his arm.

He understood her squeeze of affection, "Let's partake of a meal and a romp soon after."

THIRTY SEVEN ✭

Rebeka was just leaving the Celeste, with the children holding her hands as they started down the gangway. As she looked up from the two children, she saw Katherine at the bottom waiting a turn to come aboard. The two women knew of one another, but had not before spoken. Rebeka said, "Good morn to you. You're the Pilot's wife, Katherine, are you not?"

"Yes, I am Katherine, Jim Barnstable's wife. How is it aboard this day?"

"It was quiet until my children started making a fuss. They are just hungry, so we're on our way home."

"Jim and I have walked past your cottage on the hill. It's lovely."

"Yes, it is a nice cottage. . . . I'm sorry I don't know where you live."

"Jim and I have been paying a landlord for the use of a peasants home. But, now with his new position as a ship's Pilot, I'm thinking we need to find something more suitable."

With her children tugging at her hands to go home, Rebeka decided, "Katherine, when you're done here on the ship today, why don't you join me for tea?"

Katherine smiled broadly. "Rebeka, I would love to have tea with you. I shant be but a short time aboard with Jim. I'll try to be along shortly."

Rebeka had fed the children, then laid them down for a nap. They were past the age of daily naps, and growing much too fast, but sometimes she needed a bit of time to herself and the children were in need of some rest. This was one of those days and the children accepted the nap readily. Just as she came down the stairs, she heard the knock at her door.

As she opened the door she said, "Please do come in Katherine."

"Thank you." She carried a small package, and she followed Rebeka to her kitchen then sat at a round hardwood table. Rebeka brought two small cups and poured tea for the both of them. Katherine said, "Oh, I brought some sweet biscuits from the Franklin Bakery. They are quite good."

"Yes, they are. We have them on occasion ourselves."

As the two of them chatted about the ship and its coming voyage, Katherine confessed, "My late husband was lost at sea. He fell off a yard, over the side, and was not found."

"I'm so sorry, Katherine."

"No matter now, with Jim and all. Still I have to wonder how long he will be gone on his voyages."

"I'm sure that if he remains with Humphry Limited, that his voyages will be shorter than most men who go to sea."

"That would please me, but why would his being on one of Mister Humphry's ships be any different?"

"Richard likes the short trips so as to make a quick profit. The things he seeks are easily found, and have a high market ready on the ship's return. He only plans on his ships making as short a voyage as possible. It seems to be working quite well, too." It was silent between them for a few moments, then Rebeka asked, "I'm a bit curious Katherine, what kind of dwelling are you and Jim going to seek for your new home?"

"I'd love to have a house, and Jim is as excited as I am, but they are too large for just the two of us. But, a good cottage, at a reasonable cost is more likely what we'll look for, though they are not easy to come by."

"I know. John and I looked for over a year to find this one. It has been cared for, and in good order. Now I'm trying to convince him we need to purchase a house. Not a large garish house, but something larger than our cottage. As a ship's Captain he will be expected to entertain those in this new social circle." As she looked at Katherine over the rim of her cup, she saw her eyes shift to another place. She was thinking of something in her own life. It was moments before Katherine spoke.

"Rebeka, I'd not thought about social circles. I've not been a part of them in the past, but now that Jim is a ship's Pilot, is he equal to a ship's Captain?"

"Hmm. I don't know. It is a position of social standing. It has to be similar. Perhaps we can find out."

"And, your cottage. . . .what will become of it when you move to a larger house?"

Rebeka smiled, she understood Katherine's motive for the inquiry. "We'd have no further use for it. Would you be Interested in having it?"

"I am. It would suit us well."

"I think we should discuss this further. Perhaps when our men folk are at sea, so they cannot interfere with foolish questions."

Both women smiled as they raised a tea cup to their lips. Both were thinking of the future.

THIRTY EIGHT ✶

Winter had passed easily. There had been little snow, and the river had frozen, but even that lasted but a short time. It was the first week of May and the weather was warmer than in years past. The two ships and their crews were ready for the upcoming voyage. The Quest was moored to the wharf, and the Celeste had anchored out in Still Water Bay the day before.

The crew of the Celeste had been aboard, John was delivered to his ship early this morning after having said goodbye to his wife and children. He was thinking of taking his son, Tim, along on a voyage before long. He would speak to Rebeka on his return from this trip.

To his new First Mate on the Quest, Ian said, "Mister Rankin."

"Aye, Sir."

"Signal the Celeste to weigh anchor."

"Aye, Sir." He walked to the starboard rail, raised a pistol and fired one shot. Then he and the Captain waited until the crew of the Celeste answered in kind.

On the Celeste, Captain John Davis gave the order to his First Mate, "Mister Mathews, acknowledge the message from the Quest." Then, as his first sea order, he ordered his Bosun, "Mister Harmon, man the capstan to weigh anchor, then raise your sails to make way."

The Bosun assembled his men and they slowly began the back breaking work of walking the capstan around to pull the large anchor free of the mud on the bottom of the bay. When it came free, two crewmen pulling buckets of sea water up from the bay washed the mud from the anchor flukes. As they did this, the crew of the Celeste quickly raised two Jibs and the Spanker. Shortly after that the fore-Mainsail and Mainsail were hauled up and the ship was making its way out to sea.

John spoke again to his Mate, "Mister Mathews."

"Aye, Sir."

"You'll have to keep a measure on the amount of canvas you have up."

"Aye, Sir. Understood, Sir."

At John's side stood Jim Barnstable, the ship's Pilot. "Why would he measure the ship's canvas, Captain?"

John smiled. "Not as in 'what size is the canvas,' but in how much sail we have up at any time. You see, the Celeste is a faster ship than the Quest and we'll need to match her speed with our own." Then he continued, "Do you have a favored course laid out for the voyage, Jim?"

"I do, Captain."

The Mate was standing near the Helmsman, Pink Lark, as he heard the Captain once again.

"Mister Mathews. After you've cleared land's end, and set your watches, will you fetch Mister Barnstable and join me in my cabin?"

"Aye, Sir."

"Jim, have your charts ready to study when we meet."

"Aye, Sir."

John went below to his cabin. He would consult his own charts, and his preferred course to follow, before the Mate and Pilot joined him.

*   *   *

On the Quest the order had been given to bring in the mooring lines and to loose the ship from the wharf. With Jibs and Spanker raised to help the Helmsman get steerage, the Mainsails were raised as the ship began to move. As she began to make way, the Captain, Ian Hawkins, spoke to his First Mate, "Mister Rankin."

"Aye, Sir."

"It seems you've an extra man aboard."

"Aye, Sir. I'll see to it, Sir."

"Very well. When you've set the watches, join me in my cabin when you're free."

"Aye, Sir."

As Ian was pulling his cabin door closed behind him, he heard the splash and he looked out his aft portal. He could see a man in the cold water of the bay yelling at the ship's First Mate, his arm in the air as he shook his fist in apparent anger. Ian just smiled.

Out of his view, a small skiff quickly made its way toward the man in the water. A blanket awaited him, and soon after, a warming fire and a mug of hot broth.

THIRTY NINE ✫

The ship's bell sounded eight bells as John, Jim Barnstable and the First Mate, Daniel Mathews stood on the bridgedeck. They were watching the Bo`sun, Mister Timothy Rawlin, working the on watch crew. They were coiling down lines and trimming sails.

John looked at the wake of the ship. It was leaving very little wake as it moved through the quiet sea. "We're making good time on our passage."

Daniel liked the feel of the Celeste. "She fits the water well, she does."

John smiled. "Yes, she does sail well."

"The weather's been kind to us, too, Captain."

"Yes it has, though that's not usually the case In this part of the sea."

"Nay, tis not. I hope it will hold."

John had a quick look at the sky, the weather had been nice for the two days since they'd left home waters. "I see no reason for it to change, least ways not for a day or two."

"It would be a welcome voyage if we'd make the whole of it in fair weather."

"One direction or the other we'll have to pay Neptune his due."

As the three men watched, the Bo`sun came aft to where they stood, gave John a short two finger salute, his fingers barely touching his forehead. "May I have a word with you, Sir."

"Surely, Mister Rawlin." He walked him a short distance away from the others to give him some privacy should he need it.

"I'm thankin' you kindly, Sir, for the position of Bo'sun aboard your ship, Sir."

"No need, you've been of value to me in the past, and I know you can handle the men and the ship."

"Still, Sir. It's an honor to be aboard the Celeste, and me missus is mighty proud too, Sir."

FORTY ✫

It was mid week as Rebeka sat across from Margaret in her parlor, each sipping at a cup of tea. The subject of their conversation was about Katherine's social standing, now that her husband was a ship's Pilot.

"Margaret, I've no knowledge of Katherine's position. She's my friend and, like myself, we find we need help from our friends. I have no idea how I would have managed without your help in my life. You've been such a dear." She also knew that though Margaret was a gracious hostess and enjoyed the arts, she had a hidden side to her. She could also be a rebellious person, someone who would go against the establishment when, or if, she felt it was needed.

"Yes, she is on middle ground, so to speak. She's been widowed and she's been a hair dresser to Elizabeth and myself. Still she is my friend as well. I, too, have no knowledge of her social position, unless we make it our business. But, Rebeka, she cannot entertain in a peasants home. She simply cannot."

"Would a nice cottage be acceptable?"

Margaret was silent for a few seconds, then said, "I think so, if it is as nice as your own."

"I think they're planning on obtaining one. A nice one, and one I'm familiar with."

The two of them sat for a few moments, sipping quietly, both thinking of what could be done. Margaret smiled. "Rebeka, most of the women in our group started out in much lower social standings than those we now hold."

"Yes, I know. Elizabeth was but a wife to a shipping assistant in the beginning. Then Richard purchased his first packet ship, and things just seemed to fall in place for them. You mentioned something about making Katherine's social standing our business?"

Margaret smiled. "I think we should have a high tea one afternoon. I'll invite all of the merchant's wives, you, of course, and Katherine, and I'll offer an invitation to Missus Lissa Franklin as well."

"Do you mean the wife of the baker, Tom Franklin?"

"Yes, that's the woman. Do you know her?"

"Not really, though I met her husband while he was aboard the Quest."

"They have done quite well as merchants. I understand he is going to open his second shop soon."

Rebeka felt sure that the issue of Katherine was now in good hands. "Margaret, thank you for your kindness to me, and your thoughtfulness for others." She was surprised at her own thinking about Katherine and her manipulation of the events, and she wondered if she herself was becoming, 'uppity.'

"Rebeka, everyone who knows me, knows I'm outspoken. Some even refer to me as brazen, or worse, but though I'm quiet about things, I am privy to a great deal of personal information. Most of those women we socialize with would not have me starting gossip around towne."

"Could that gossip include me?" Rebeka was startled to think that Margaret would say things about her.

"Ah, you my Dear, are still a mystery to me."

"I think I should keep it that way."

FORTY ONE ✶

Rebeka had a new dress, as did Katherine. The two of them had never dressed like this in their entire lives. It took them all morning to do each other's hair and to get dressed properly for high tea with Margaret and the other ladies that were to attend. A noise drew Katherine's attention, and she had looked out of Rebeka's window. "Rebeka our carriage is here."

Both women were apprehensive as they exited the carriage. The driver offered his hand to each of them in turn. Each carried a parasol decorated with floral scenes, though they were not needed. When they arrived at Margaret's door, Jesselyn smiled at them as she opened the door and bade them to enter. Because of her past history with Katherine, these were two women she could relate to. When the two of them walked into Margaret's parlor, every eye in the room turned their way.

Margaret quickly walked to their side, and then made her way with them around the room as she introduced them to the others already in attendance. The introductions went smoothly, and each woman acknowledged them both. In less than five minutes they were talking with others as if they'd known one another for years. Lissa had arrived before anyone else had and she had her driver bring in many of her husbands latest sweet rolls and cakes made just for the occasion. She and Margaret had agreed upon this arrangement before hand. Jesselyn saw to it that Rebeka, Katherine, and Lissa, were better served than any of the others. She could speak freely with these three. They were closer to her kind.

The small cakes were cut into small servings and quickly disappeared. The sweet rolls were a new item and were welcomed eagerly. The sweet biscuits were adorned with a cinnamon spice recently acquired by the bakery. Lissa saw sales booming as she watched and listened to the conversations about the goodies being served.

FORTY TWO ✴

Francisco DeMetrito, the spokesman for the group of vineyard owners, was entertaining the Captains of the Celeste and the Quest in his home on the evening before their departure for home. His wife, Rosa, had seen to it that the meal had been exquisite and it was served in their formal dining room. Several of the best wines from their vineyards had been opened for tasting.

Francisco had been uncomfortable and apprehensive all evening. These two men had come from England to purchase every bottle of last years wine crop, and those bottles now rested in the ship's holds. The purchase of these wines had not produced a profit for the vineyards on this sale. The money received had just paid for the bottles used.

Francisco had spoken harshly with the vineyard owners who had taken advantage of the last ship's captain from England. The owners had come away from the meeting with him with a better understanding of how their actions could effect the entire economy of the Island. Francisco did not want to anger these men, as they represented an association of long term business dealings, but the others had not been completely honest in their dealings with the Captain of the Lady Ann.

Francisco had not been part of the previous sale, nor of this one, but he felt guilty because he knew the wines sold before were of inferior quality. The vineyard owners were happy because they had been paid in full with gold coins. Even yet, as far as he knew, still nothing had been said about the wine's condition.

As the evening drew to an end Ian asked, "Francisco, why is it you did not sell us any of your wines?"

"I am sorry, I simply do not have any wine from that season that I judge to be worthwhile to market."

John almost laughed, but managed only a smile. He liked this man. He had honor. He would see to it that most of their future purchases would be from him first. As they readied to leave, John said, "Thank you for a very pleasant evening, Mister De Metrito. I expect we will be doing business with you again."

Francisco could not stand it any longer. "Gentlemen, I'm curious. Why is it you agreed to purchase every last bottle of last years vintage when it is known that the wines were inferior."

Ian and John had made an agreement before they left the ships. They had agreed they would not mention the condition of the wines, though they had expressed a curiosity between themselves as to whether it would be mentioned during dinner.

John, now taking the lead, said, "Senior De Metrito, we should thank you for the wines currently in our hold. We made a fortune on our investment last season. We expect to do as well this season."

Francisco was caught off guard, his head twisting slightly as he turned to look at John, and an eyebrow raised as he looked straight into John's eyes. He said, "How is that possible? The wines were of poor quality."

"Oh, yes. They were, indeed, poor wines, but they were excellent vinegars."

Francisco sat up much straighter, the fingers of his left hand coming up to his chin as he thought about what had just been said. Then a smile appeared. The smile was replaced by a roar of laughter.

FORTY THREE ✶

The Celeste had been the first to have her cargo of wines loaded aboard, and when her hold had been filled, the crews loaded the hold of the Quest. Then the crews were given time ashore, leaving only a skeleton crew aboard each ship to look after the ship's needs. Then those men were given time on the beach. John and Ian had enjoyed the evening before at the DeMetrito's home. Rosa had seen to their every need during dinner, and Francisco made sure they would call on him anytime in the future for anything they might need. It had been an unwritten agreement, but all three men knew most of their business would be through him.

John and Ian were standing on the quay, each looking at their respective crews making last minute adjustments to rigging and to storage of the ship's cargo. Ian was rubbing his left arm as he said, "We'll leave on the morning tide, John."

John had noticed Ian rubbing his arm, and that he had been doing this often during the morning. "Aye, though it will be early, there should be enough light."

Ian's head swept the skies, "Weather seems fair, but it can change around here in a matter of hours."

"Well, we're ready, though low in the water with the amount of cargo we've aboard. Still, that shouldn't be a problem. Both ships are sound."

"I'm going aboard the Quest now. Why don't you join me this evening for some libation?"

"I look forward to that." Then, out of curiosity he said, "Ian, is your arm bothering you?"

"Yes. . .a bit. Seems to be tingling. I'm sure it'll stop."

'I'll see you around six bells then?"

"Yes, that's a good time. Dinner will be over and the crew settled in for the evening. Until then."

Just as both men turned to go to their respective ships, a carriage came rushing toward them. It came to a stop at the gangway of the Quest. The driver jumped down, and ran up the gangway to the deck. They watched as the First Mate, Rankin, pointed to the two Captains standing on the quay.

He arrived at their sides, saying, "Captains, I am to provide you with some wines for your personal use. Francisco De Metrito sent some from his personal wine cellar. With each you will find his letter on how to best enjoy them. He apologizes for not being able to bring them himself."

Ian said, "Please tell him thank you, and that we will drink to his health."

The driver then saw to it that there was equal share of the wines for both ships, then he left to return to the vineyard.

That evening the two of them went over the letter explaining the wines.

'Captain, I send these wines for your personal enjoyment. Each is a unique wine and deserves to be treated with respect. The Malmsey should not be opened until you are home, as it is better after having traveled. The Sercial, is still young and should be left to age at least another year. The Baul, and Maderia, can be enjoyed at your pleasure. When you again visit, we can taste some of our newest wines. I think you will find them to be very good.
Francisco DeMetrito. '

John spoke as he went over the meaning of the letter, "I think I will just wait until long after we've returned home to taste these wines. I don't think I can fully enjoy them at the time. I simply do not have enough experience to know how good they are."

"I shall do the same, John. Though I do know a good wine when I have it, I will wait as well. One day, while we are visiting, we can open one of these. We will smile knowing how we came to have them and enjoy them that much more."

FORTY FOUR ✷

Ian had been right about the weather. It stayed
fair. The ships were sailing North by Northeast on
the first of three planned tacks. They had planned
on making a port tack off the coast of Portugal
onto a Northwest by West. Once they were close
to England and still well below the Lizard, they
would tack again. This last course change would
take them nearly home.

As John came topside the second morning at sea,
the ship's crew was forward watching a pod of
whales as they passed the ship. Their long backs
humped in the water as they emptied their lungs
through the blowhole, then slipped under. The
Quest was nearly over the horizon ahead of them,
and he noted the whales seemed to be heading
directly in her direction. They too, would be
treated to the spectacle.

It was less than two hours later when his Mate
called his attention to the Quest ahead. "Captain,
the Quest is furling all sail, Sir."

John looked ahead. They had gained on the
Quest, and she was nearly dead in the water as
the last of her canvas was being furled. She was
now drifting slowly and lying broadside to the
waves and wind. "What do you make of it, Mister
Mathews?"

"I think they've a problem, Sir. Why else would they take in all sail in fair weather, Sir?"

"I think you're right. Get our canvas down, leave just enough to make way. We'll heave to off their stern quarter."

"Aye, Sir."

When the Celeste drew near the stern of the Quest, Mister Rankin, the First Mate shouted to them. John and Daniel listened carefully, then John fetched his looking glass to inspect the stern of the Quest. On careful examination, he confirmed what the Mate had said. The rudder had been lifted from its mountings. It was tilted at a slight angle. He also saw Ian leaning against the stern rail, but it was the Mate making the exchange of words, not the Captain. John gave his First Mate some instructions, then went to talk with Jim Barnstable.

All sails on the Celeste were stowed temporarily while a small boat was lowered from her main deck with a strong rowing crew aboard. Jim went down the rope ladder. It took them longer than John expected, but they rowed to the Quest. Jim took a letter to Ian with John's recommendations. Shortly after Jim had boarded the Quest, Mister Rankin shouted Ian's approval to the plan.

The skiff returned with a small line. Attached to this line was a larger line, and to that another larger mooring line. The skiff was brought aboard the Celeste and the lines were pulled aboard using the capstan. Though seldom used, it was the longest mooring line aboard the Quest, commonly used to pull her from a close anchorage to the wharf at home. When the end was aboard the Celeste, a bridal was made from another line aboard. The whole arrangement tied them to the stern of the Quest. The Mates shouted orders to their independent crews and all was readied for an unusual undertaking.

First the lower fore Mainsail on the Quest was raised and the ship began to make way. With her helm tied amidship and pulling the Celeste, the drag of the Celeste pulled her stern around. The crew of the Celeste hoisted a double reefed Spanker sail, and one reefed outer Jib. As the two ships got underway, Jim Barnstable gave signals from either the port or starboard sides of the stern rail of the Quest. Daniel Mathews relayed orders for course changes to either port or starboard of the Celeste. The Celeste's movement from side to side was steering the Quest, as if it was a large rudder, on her chosen course. Their intended destination was Lisbon, Portugal.

When John summoned the Bo'sun, on the skiffs return, he'd learned of the problem on board the Quest. As he understood it, a whale coming to the surface right under the rudder post had dislodged the bottom of the rudder and it had jammed. It could be fixed, but not easily while at sea.

John looked at his charts of the entrance to the large open Bay of Lisbon. There were a few dangers he knew about, having been here before and if they stayed off the beach far enough it would be a safe journey. As the ship doing the steering for the Quest, he had little control. In case of a pending disaster he knew he could slip the towing rig and bear his ship away. In his mind he knew it would be better to lose one ship instead of two. He knew Captain Hawkins would agree.

During the night they had used lanterns as signals, and at dawn the coastline of Portugal was in sight. As John watched ahead, it looked as if they might be going too close to land's end as they entered. The opening was large, but it seemed as though Jim was taking the shortest route in.

*   *   *

Ian was not feeling well, and he had to trust his First Mate and the Pilot, to maneuver the ship inside the bay safely. He stayed below because when he'd last looked at the chosen course, he felt even worse as the excitement grew within him at the possible danger.

None of them knew that Jim had been here before. There were dangers and most were known, but he knew of a few others, where they were, and how to avoid them. As they neared his intended turning point, he gave the signal from the starboard rail. He wanted the Celeste to pull the stern of the Quest in that direction and by his calculations, they would soon round the next point and could then anchor nearly anywhere. Jim had a man forward sounding with the lead line as they passed over a shoal not shown on charts, one that shifted with the seasons. He listened intently as he heard the man calling aft to him, "By the mark four, Sir." And within seconds, "By the mark four, Sir."

Jim's eyes had scanned the beaches and he felt sure they were at low tide now. When he heard it again, "By the mark four, Sir." he went to the aft rail to make his signal.

                    *   *   *

John gave the helmsman the order as relayed by his First Mate forward in the bow and he watched as the Celeste forcibly pulled the stern of the Quest to starboard. They were entering the bay and all had gone well. His chart had been marked by Jim and it showed a large rock that would be awash at low tide. Jim referred to it as the 'Widow Maker'. He'd not seen any sign of it as they made the turn. Now, some two hours later a swinging lantern amidships of the stern signaled that he was to drop the tow line.

When he felt the Celeste respond to the loss of the load, he gave the order to veer off and prepare to drop the port anchor. As they passed the stern of the Quest he saw Ian standing at the stern bridgedeck rail giving them a sign of well done. The anchor of the Quest smacked the water at the same second. When the ships were safely anchored, the crew of the Celeste put their skiff over the side and John and his First Mate, Daniel Mathews, were delivered to the Quest's weather deck.

FORTY FIVE ✸

When John gained his footing on the deck of the Quest the Mate, Mister Rankin, met him and said quietly, "Captain Davis, Captain Hawkins is below in his cabin, Sir."

John looked at him questioningly. "Is there a problem with the Captain?"

"He's been off his feet, Sir. He's not well, Sir."

John started aft slowly so he and the Mate could walk along and speak quietly. His own First Mate, Mister Mathews, could hear the conversation, and John didn't mind, but he wanted to keep it from the rest of the crew. "What have you noticed about the Captain?"

"I'm not sure of it, Sir. But, he's been favorin' his left side some, and stayin' below, mostly. I go to his cabin to get his sailing orders, Sir."

"Okay, I'll go report myself aboard. If you'll tell Mister Mathews the problem with your steering we'll see about getting repairs started."

As the two Mates stopped to talk, John went below. He stopped and knocked at the elaborately carved door to the Captain's quarters.

He heard the customary, "Come." But the voice seemed quieter than normal, as if it lacked the ring of authority.

When John opened the door, Ian stood slowly. "Ah, John. Come in and sit down."
Then he, himself, sat again. "John, you and your crew did well in helping steer the Quest to safety."

"Yes, it did go well. Do you have any idea of what happened?" He wanted to be sure Ian was aware of the ship's condition.

"I think a whale broached under the rudder, and it lifted at the same time, pushing it out of the rudder post mounting. I had the crew tie the helm off. It can be fixed, but it will be much easier here at anchor."

As Ian spoke, John noticed his words were coming off his tongue with some difficulty.
"Ian, you're not well, are you?"

Ian's jaw line tightened as he fought with the answer. He knew that this was one man he had to trust and be truthful with. "No, I'm not." He looked at John as he continued. "I think it might be my ticker." His right hand moved to his chest.

Both of them knew this could be a serious problem. "What do you propose, Ian?"

"I don't want to give up command of the ship as we are so near home, but I need to arrange something."

John sat quietly while Ian told him how he felt, then he said, "Suppose I leave Daniel Mathews, my First Mate, aboard with you. He and your First Mate, Raymond Rankin, can get the ship home. You stay aboard and in command, and I'll follow along in the Celeste. Should it be needed I can come aboard anytime you might need me."

"Which of the two men has the most experience?"

"Daniel does."

"What will you do for a First Mate if I keep Mister Mathews?"

"I'll take Timothy Rawlins, your Bo`sun."

Ian was still for some time. John didn't rush him. "Let me think on this John."

"Very well, Sir. I'll go see that the rudder repairs are taken care of."

Very quietly, Ian said, "Thank you, John."

"Aye, Sir."

FORTY SIX ✮

Top side, John spoke with the two First Mates. They all agreed on the best way to repair the rudder, and they were to start the next morning. Then he took the two men to the privacy of the bow to tell them about the crew changes he planned.

"Mister Rankin, Mister Mathews will move his duffle aboard the Quest. The two of you will be responsible for taking her home." He watched the two men's eyes light up as they exchanged glances. "The Captain will remain in command, but the two of you will be running the ship. . . .Do you understand my meaning?"

They were solemn as they answered, "Aye, Sir."

"Mister Mathews, you will be responsible for the major decisions, but you will work with Mister Rankin. Mister Rankin, you will remain in control of the crew as First Mate. Is this agreeable to the two of you?"

Daniel asked, "What are my duties to be then, Sir?"

"You will see that Captain Hawkins orders are carried out as he wishes. If need be, you might make suggestions when you feel they are needed."

"I'm to be caught in the middle, as it were, Sir?"

John smiled. "Aye, and it may not be an easy position."

Daniel understood his role as a go between. He did not know what might come his way if he made a mistake but he was willing to take that chance. "I'll do it, Sir."

John looked at Raymond, "And, will this arrangement work for you?"

"I'll be happy just to keep my position as Mate. I've no desire to do what you're asking of Mister Mathews."

John was relieved, he thought he'd made the correct choice before telling these two men of his decision. "Very well. Mister Mathews you should tell the Bo`sun, Rawlins, to pack his gear. He's to come aboard the Celeste in your place. This will bring it to this crews attention that you have some authority aboard the Quest. Mister Rankin, you should go along as well. If anyone questions anything, you will be there to back up Mister Mathews."

Both men gave him a short salute. Then he added, "Mister Mathews, you will need to return to the Celeste to pack your gear so you can move aboard the Quest."

Raymond said, "I'll order a boat to take Mister Mathews to the Celeste and back. Then I'll get the crew to make ready the things we'll need for the work on the morrow."

FORTY SEVEN ✱

As the ship's bell tolled eight bells at the turn of
the watch, the crew of the Quest was preparing
the block and tackles for the day's work. The
topside blocks were tied with strong lines looped
around the mizzen mast near the helm and at
deck level. This shared the load equally to the
ship's hull. Skiffs from both the Quest and the
Celeste were standing by off the stern of the
Quest. In one of the skiffs, Bo`sun Rawlins
waited. He'd volunteered to go over the side if
needed. Only he knew of the danger to himself.
He could not let himself get too tired.

The four fall blocks and lines were rigged low over
the sides, one on each side of the ship. Each had
a hook at the bottom of the lower block. Two
seamen had spent most of the night building a
long web strap of closely woven rope. It was to be
looped over the hooks and slipped under the
bottom of the rudder as a lifting support. When all
hands were ready, John looked at Ian and said,
"On your order, Sir."

Ian had only come topside to show the crew he
was still in command of his ship, though many
had heard rumors of his ill health.

He observed the preparations, and approved of
the procedure. He nodded his head. "Very well,
Mister Davis. Get it done."

John turned to the Mates. "Mister Rankin, Mister Mathews, you may begin."

"I'll be in my cabin if you need me, John."

"Very well, Sir."

The work went well. The steering cables had been removed from the top of the rudder so the rudder was free to move about. The crew had been divided into port and starboard work parties and were being refereed in that manner. First Mate Mathews stayed aft on the bridgedeck to oversee the work topside, and First Mate Rankin had taken his position in one of the skiffs aft of the ship's stern.

Daniel gave his first order to the Bo`sun, "Port and starboard, lift some." The blocks creaked with the load, but raised the rudder slightly. Then it was cleated off as the crew waited for the next command.

Word came up from the steering cable compartment. All was well in there and Raymond indicated everything was well, below, on the waterline. But he added, "Just lift on the starboard side this time."

Daniel answered, "Aye." Again, the order went, "Starboard, lift some." The rudder raised a bit more, but this time the bottom of it shifted slightly to starboard. As it did, all hands in the boats yelled in unison.

Everything was checked and, as before, all positions reported all was well, but Raymond called up, "Mister Mathews, the rudder stock has cleared the keel, it needs only to be moved to starboard some to be seated home"

"Aye, Mister Rankin." Then Daniel gave the order, "Port, ease off some." The bottom of the rudder shifted to starboard slightly, but not quite enough.

When it was determined everything was still being moved without any problems, the two Mates issued orders to move the rudder until it was right over the stock's seat in the keel. It needed just a bit more movement, but the Mates were afraid it would move too much. They feared it would move past the position it required to seat properly, then they'd have to jockey it back and forth, again and again.

First Mate Rankin said to the Bo`sun, "Mister Rawlins, if you've a bar to pry the rudder stock a bit, do you think you could budge it into place?"

Timothy could see the bottom of the rudder stock in the clear seawater, and it only needed a bit of a shove. "Aye, Sir. If you've a bar long enough, I can put it in place and the crew in the skiff can help pull the top of it, Sir."

A prying bar made from straight grained oak, with a forged steel end, was lowered over the stern. A rope tied through a hole in one end held it in case it was dropped. The Bo`sun, dressed in his woollies, went into the water. It was a shock to him, but it was not as cold as he thought it might be. Still, he'd need to work quickly. He went under water to work the end of the bar into the best position. He placed it between the keel and the front of the rudder stock. Then he signaled with his hand above the surface to pull it to starboard. It moved, but the bar came out. It had to be raised a bit, then pushed back in place.

He had to surface, catch his breath while holding onto the side of the skiff. Being down under the water as long as he could, had taken a toll on him. The Mate asked, "Are you well, Mister Rawlins?"

He wasn't, but he replied, "I can finish the job, Sir." Then before anything more could be said, he went under again.

It took four tries to complete the task, but finally the rudder dropped into position. When Timothy was pulled aboard the skiff, he was exhausted and very cold. The First Mate ordered the skiff to take him back to the Celeste and the boat crew to see he was warmed.

John watched as the skiff returned to the Celeste. He noted that the Bo`sun didn't climb out of the boat, he was lifted and carried aboard. He would check on the man when he returned aboard later in the day.

*   *   *

It took the remainder of the day to replace the steering cables and make sure the rudder was working properly. When everything had been taken care of, he reported to Ian in his cabin.

"It went well and I think it will stay in place, though it should be gone over when we are home and she can be put up on the dry."

"I agree, it will need to be tended, as it could be a danger to the ship. John, thank you for seeing to its repair."

"I only observed, you've a good crew aboard."

"Yes, and I'm impressed with Mister Mathews. He's a good Mate to have aboard."

FORTY EIGHT ★

When John returned to the Celeste, he asked one of the seamen, "Mister Hurley, how is Bo`sun Rawlins?"

Jim Hurley had served on other ships belonging to Humphry Limited, but this was his first time with John Davis. "He's come around Sir, though still very tired, he is."

"You say, 'come around,' as if he had some trouble?"

Jim Hurley shifted on his feet. He didn't want to tell his Captain what had happened, but he knew he had to. "Well, Sir, he'd had a fit, Sir. I put a piece of line between his teeth to keep him from biting his tongue, Sir."

John stood still. He did not say a word as he digested what had been told to him. Then, "Has this happened before?"

"Not that I know of, Sir."

"How is it you knew what to do?"

"I've seen it with others, before, Sir."

"How many others know about Mister Rawlin's trouble?"

"Just the boat crew, Sir."

"Let's keep it that way."

"Aye, Sir."

"It was good of you to help him."

"He's me shipmate, Sir."

"I'll talk to him later. You can return to your duties if you are still on watch."

"Thank you, Sir. And, Sir, if you don't mind, Sir. It'd please me, Sir, if he doesn't know I told you about him, Sir."

John smiled, "He'll not hear it from me."

Jim Hurley started to leave, then faltered, "It's not really the work of the devil, is it, Sir?"

"Those who would have you believe so, still think the world is flat."

FORTY NINE ✶

Late that day John found his Bo`sun topside attending to his duties. "Mister Rawlins, join me in my cabin when you go off watch."

"Aye aye, Sir. At eight bells, Sir?"

"At eight bells."

It took only a few minutes after the ship's bell sounded the final gong, and the ship's crews changed watches, before the knock came at his door. "Come in."

It was apparent to John that Timothy was still tired. He needed more rest and John would see that he got the time he needed whenever possible. "Please sit down."

John didn't ask, he just got up and poured them both a mug of rum. As he handed one to his Bo`sun, he said, "Are you feeling better, Mister Rawlins?"

His Bo`sun tried to appear calm. Still, he gathered himself up in the hard chair, as if he was ready to go take on any task needed, but he was failing in both. "Aye, Sir. Never better, Sir."

He sipped at the rum, and it did help him compose himself, the feeling warming him all of the way down to the gullet.

He wanted to appear as if he was comfortable. He was none of these things.

John knew better, and decided to put it to him blankly, "Have you suffered with the 'fits' since you were young?"

From the comment about his youth, Timothy knew, now, that his Captain was an informed man. He knew of these things, so he spoke more freely, "Aye, Sir, but most of the time I've no problem, unless I let myself get too tired, or too excited, Sir"

John knew the potential danger of a man in the rigging falling to his death, or simply endangering others at a critical time when your physical strength was needed the most. He could not take that chance, at least not for a prolonged period of time. That was why he'd made his decision before he spoke to his Bo`sun. "You know I cannot keep you on as a Mate. It will be too much for you over time."

Timothy had known for years that this day would come, he just didn't want it to happen this way. "I'm sorry if I've let you down, Sir."

"Timothy, you haven't let me down. I just have to find something else for you to do."

Timothy was surprised by the friendly way his Captain spoke to him, and the fact that he would try to keep him employed. "I can do many things, Captain. I learn things fast, I do."

John gave considerable thought to this man's position aboard the Celeste before he answered. "I'm sure you can do most anything, and we've but a short voyage home. Do you think you can carry out your duties for the rest of the voyage?"

He brightened, "Aye, Sir. I can, Sir."

John was sure the man would do everything in his power to pull his weight and to fulfill his role as Bo`sun. "Okay, I'm going to keep you as my Bo`sun, but if you get to the place where you question your own abilities, you must be honest with me, and tell me straight away."

"You've me word on it, Sir."

FIFTY ✷

The day before they left Portugal, John spoke with his Bo'suns. "Captain Hawkins has asked for Mister Mathews to stay aboard the Quest in case they have any more trouble with their steering. Because of this, we do not have an acting First Mate aboard. You two will have to work together better than you ever have before. I'll keep a closer eye on things as well, and if you need me for anything, day or night, come to my cabin to fetch me. Together, with your help, we can finish this voyage safely."

Both Bo'suns knew this to be an unusual condition on any ship. In a sense they were both going to be acting First Mates. They also knew that there had been many men move up in rank in the past months, and if all went well they, too, stood a chance at bettering themselves. Humphry Limited was known as a company to look after its own.

On leaving Portugal, John gave the order, "Mister Harmon, our course is to be Nor' by Nor' West."

"Aye, Sir." Harmon turned to face the Helmsman and repeated the order, "Mister Swit. Take her to Nor' by Nor' West."

"Aye, Sir. Nor' by Nor' West, Sir." The ship was almost already on that course as she exited the bay. It took little work for the crew to square the yards to the ship's slight change in her course.

Less than two days from home, a storm started to brew. It was forming to the west of their position. Still, the timing was good, as both ships changed course to North East by East. They ran under full sail downwind, homeward bound. This tack would lead them nearly to their home port. A final change of course would take them into the bay.

* * *

The Quest led the way into the bay, which was expected. Word had come from a villager on the coast that the two ships had been sighted earlier, and the wharves were crowded with townspeople on their arrival. Many of those watching just came to see the spectacle of the Quest as it bore down on the Humphry wharf. Then, at the last minute, it seemed to lose all headway and simply tie up. Normally, her crew would need only to heave lines to men standing at the ready ashore who would berth her along side the heavy timbers.

The wives and girlfriends of the crews were waiting anxiously. Richard Humphry was away on business, so he was absent from the throngs of people. Margaret, Rebeka, and Katherine sat in Margaret's carriage and appeared to be exchanging the latest gossip. Each, in reality was excited because the ship and their men folk were home. Before Margaret had left her bedroom, she'd placed her gift from Katherine away, amongst her under things.

When the Quest did not sail up to the wharf, but instead doused all sail and then dropped her anchor, close, but out from the wharf, it surprised everyone. This was not Captain Hawkins way of doing things. It simply wasn't what they expected. Still, the ships were home and apparently safe. The ship would be pulled by long boats and crews, to the wharf or warped into the wharf with the long mooring lines when it was ready.

In short order, skiffs from both ships were lowered, but the one from the Quest was first at the wharf. The one from the Celeste followed close behind, and Captain Hawkins waited on the wharf for Captain Davis to land. "John, will you attend to our business. I feel I must go home."

"I'll take care of it Ian. Let me walk with you to your carriage. Should you need my arm, we can act as though we are conversing on a ship's matter."

"Very well ,John, and thank you."

As the two men walked to Ian's carriage, they did chat about what was needed for the ships the following day. On arrival at his carriage, Rebeka and Katherine alighted. John helped Ian into the carriage, and the wives felt something was amiss. John stepped up to speak quietly, "Margaret, Ian is not feeling well. You should send for his physician, straight away."

He could see the fear in her eyes, so he said, "I do believe he is not in any immediate danger, but he needs his rest. He will explain things to you, and about our trying trip."

She nodded her head, then ordered the driver to move on quickly.

He took Rebeka into his arms, hugged her, and kissed her passionately, then said, "Well, my Love, I have a few things to take care of. Would you care to accompany me?"

She smiled warmly, "Of course dear Husband. . . .But what illness is it that has its hold on Ian?"

"I can only guess, I suspect it may be his heart. Of course no one is to know of this, dear Wife."

"Oh, goodness, John. That is not good news at all."

"We'll know in a few days. At least we got him home."

Jim and Katherine had already left to go home themselves. John saw to the ships immediate needs, arranged for the duty watch crews on board both ships, then he, himself, went home.

His children were being cared for by an elderly woman from down the lane. When they saw their father, she could not contain them. John became a beehive of activity with the kissing and hugging from the youngsters. They would be up late this night listening to the latest stories of the sea, and he would have to tell the ghost ship story again as they liked it the best. Though it had taken place the year before, they still wanted to hear it again.

The hour had grown late and she hated to wake the three of them, but the children had fallen asleep in the big chair within their father's arms, and it was time for them to retire. Rebeka too, needed some quiet time with John.

"John. . . .John. . . .Her hand shook him a little harder. John. . ."

"Wha'. . . Oh, Becky my love, we must have . . . "

"Yes, you did. Now it's my turn."

He smiled, "Ah, Dear Wife, my brief nap will have served us well."

After the children were bedded down, the two of them undressed each other. Then they played for hours.

FIFTY ONE ✳

It took longer to unload the ships than it took to load them. In Madeira the ship's crew had helped the workers from the vineyards to load the ship's cargo. Here, at home, the crews had been paid off, and the men from Richard's warehouses did the unloading. The regular crewmen would be asked to join the ship on its next voyage, and some would accept. A few would have already gone on to other vessels.

Both First Mates had asked for time away, but would return soon. As the ship's business was under control, their family needs came first and the two men were paid off.

The only men aboard the ships were Bo'suns Timothy Rawlins, from the Celeste, and two seamen, and Raymond Rankin, from the Quest, and one seaman who had nowhere else to go.

Each of the Bo'suns were responsible for the well being of the ship. The Quest was due to be put onto the hard and dried out to make permanent repairs to the rudder stock. Raymond Rankin had been asked to oversee the ship's movement on a daily basis.

The Captain would normally be involved in this as well, but there were rumors circulating about the good Captain, and no one knew any answers.

At least no one on board the ships was privy to this information.

There were merchants waiting in groups for the remainder of the ship's cargo to be unloaded on the final day. Richard Humphry was in his element among them, though he was tiring of the constant daily hassle of business. He liked making the contacts, making the sales pitch, and seeing to his office affairs. What he was having trouble with, these days, was the constant organizing it took to run the fleet of ships, though he only had five at the time.

His wife, Constance, had over the years, constantly imagined she had more illnesses coursing through her system than she really had. She conjured up every conceivable sickness she'd ever heard of. However, in the last few years she had gained considerable weight, and it was taking a toll on her well being. She could not easily get around by herself, and though she had a personal maid, Richard was in more demand at home than any time before. This too, interfered with his business routines.

Today's sales of chosen vinegar wines, was lively. Word had gotten around about the last cargo he'd sold, and how fast it had sold out completely. This time the merchants were there to purchase anything for sale. It was bedlam. Bidding began low at first. Then it simply took on a life of its own. With Richard agreeing to prices, Martin, his secretary, was writing the orders. Within three hours of the first sale, there was not a bottle left to sell.

Outside of the warehouse, some of the buyers were heard to be selling some of the vinegars they had purchased just moments before. One man had sold his entire stock, then realized he had none for himself. He had to pay dearly just to get a few bottles back.

FIFTY TWO ✷

The two men did not discuss their personal health in great detail, or family conditions, as they sipped from crystal glasses. They sat in Richard's office addressing the very situations they each faced, both laying the truth on the table, and going over what they needed in their lives.

"So, your heart is giving you some trouble now and again?"

"It's not been a problem while I've been home, Richard. Being in Margaret's care has helped a great deal. . . .More relaxed, I suppose, or maybe it's just being home."

Richard had thought much of the conversation through beforehand. He'd already planned a great deal of what he had to say. He'd even asked his wife, Constance, for her opinion. She had thought the idea was wonderful. Of course he knew she would.

"Ian, I've a proposal. I'm not the young man I used to be and I'd like to partially retire. I want to keep my hand in the business end of Humphry Limited, but I'd like to get away from the daily demands of the shipping business."

He was quiet for a moment, then continued. "I wonder, . . . would you be interested in taking on that task? It would mean you wouldn't be going to sea, and I've no doubt you would miss that part of your life, but you would be busy and share in the profits."

For Ian it was a dream come true. He, also, had grown tired of the constant trips away from home. This position would mean he could still live the good life, have a good wage, and be involved in the seaman's world. He knew he spoke too quickly, but it didn't matter. Margaret would be pleased if he accepted.

"I accept your proposal! When do we start?"

"On the morrow, if that's not to soon?"

"Excellent, my friend! Excellent!"

As they sipped their third glass of sherry, they spoke of other things, but Richard had one more concern, and he said, "You will want to consider who will be taking your place as Captain of the Quest."

"Why, John Davis, of course." He hadn't even taken time to think of his answer. It was the only logical choice.

"I suspected that would be your answer, and I approve. But then, who is to take command of the Celeste?"

Smiling, he said. "I'll speak with John about that."

FIFTY THREE ✮

The changes that took place in the following weeks were gradual. Ian had taken over a spare room in Richard's business establishment and turned it into his office. Martin found himself working for two men, but he had no problem accepting the slight difference in work loads. He also had no problem accepting an increase in wages.

John Davis easily stepped into the role of Captain of the Quest and, today, he and Ian were discussing the future Captain of the Celeste and also the fate of Mister Rawlins, the Bo`sun from the Celeste.

"Yes, John, I spoke with Richard at length about this man's abilities. His concern, and mine, is the fact that he has risen so quickly in his positions in such a short time. Is it too much too soon?"

"I too, have thought in depth about the responsibilities he will be taking on. I think he can fulfill the position, but we might help him along the way. Such as providing a Pilot on board the Celeste, one that will help his Captain advance his own skills in navigation."

"You know, of course, that Richard entertains the thought of putting a Pilot on each of his ships. He's of the opinion it helps speed the voyages, and this means a higher profit."

"I've heard that before, but we've only one Pilot now. . . . Jim Barnstable."

"Yes. William Becker is off on an adventure, somewhere to the far west, I believe. But, we can place Jim on the Celeste as long as he's needed."

Martin knocked at his door, then poked his head in. "The Gentleman is here, Sir."

"Please send him in." Ian rose from behind his desk and moved to greet him. John rose as well, but remained by his chair.

"Ah, Mister Mathews, come in, come in. Please be seated."

"Good day to you Captain Hawkins," then he turned, "and to you, Captain Davis, Sir."
He sat, but he was nervous. Something was going on and he didn't know what it might be, nor did anyone else he'd asked.

There are a few things we would like to go over with you. One of those is your feelings about Mister Barnstable."

"The Pilot, Sir?"

"Yes, the Pilot."
"I've spoken with him, Sir, but I don't really know him well."

216

"Do you feel he is qualified in his duties?"

"Oh, yes, Sir. I know something of navigation myself, but Mister Barnstable knows much more than I or many others, I'm sure. Why, just as we were going into Portugal, he pointed out the dangers to me while we were at the helm station. He reads the water better than most men I've met. Aye, Sir, a smart one, that."

Ian looked him squarely in the eyes. "Daniel, John and I have talked a great deal about you. You've impressed me from the time you first stepped aboard one of my ships. You handled the repairs in Portugal, and worked well with another man who was, in fact, your equal, but you easily took control and led the way for the repairs to get done."

"Thank you, Sir."

Then John spoke, "Daniel, you know I always relied upon your abilities. First as a Bo`sun then as my First Mate. You always handled yourself well and the men respect you. All of these things are marks of a good man of the sea. . . and. . . I believe. . .Ian has some news for you. I think you should accept what he has to offer."

Ian took over immediately. "Yes. Richard Humphry, on our recommendation, has given us the choice of offering you the position of Captain of the Celeste, if you've an interest?"

Daniel's mouth opened, no words came out, and tears appeared in the corners of his eyes. He was dumbfounded. To be offered a command of his own was one of those things a man of the sea only dreams of. He didn't have to think about it. He just didn't know what to say. He tried, but it was gibberish. "I, uh, Captain of the Celeste! Oh, my God! A ship's Captain. Oh my, oh my. . . "

John smiled at the pleasure of seeing this man in this state of mind. "Are we to assume you will accept the position?"

Daniel stood, extended his hand to both men. "Yessir. Most definitely, Sir. I'll work hard to prove you've made a good choice, Sir."

Ian said, "You've a great deal to learn, Captain, a great deal."

Just then Martin opened the door again. "The other Gentleman is here, Sir. Shall I bring him in, Sir?"

Ian said, "Yes, Martin. Please do."

When Timothy Rawlins came into the office, he wore a nervous smile. "Sirs."

After he sat in the only remaining chair, Ian spoke, "Mister Rawlins, Humphry Limited has a new position open. If you are able to fill the position as Quartermaster, it can be yours."

He felt sure this was being offered to him because of his Captain, John Davis. He looked at John, but John did not betray any emotion. Still, he was sure it was because of John's importance with the company, and their private talk aboard the Celeste. "Quartermaster, Sir?"

"Yes, It will require you to supply all of the ship's needs and to see to the loading of those ships. Martin will help you get established and, over time, teach you how to make purchases from different merchants."

"This is to be an important position, isn't it, Sir?"

John leaned forward in his chair. "Timothy, it is an important position. You do not have to accept the responsibility if you are too uncomfortable with the duties. It is something being offered to you as a faithful employee of Humphry Limited. If, at any time, you do not feel you can do the tasks asked of you, you can simply tell Captain Hawkins, here."

"What will happen to me if I can't do the job?"

Ian added, "I'll try to find something else for you."

He wasn't smiling now. His life was taking a serious turn. He said, "I would like to give it a try, Sir."

"Good. You can start on the morrow, and you will be working with the new Captain of the Celeste."

"Who might that be, Sir?"

"That is the Captain to your starboard, Mister Mathews has accepted the command."

"He jumped up, and looked at Daniel. "Blimey, Sir. Good oh, Sir." His hand shot out in a gesture of congratulations.

Daniel took his hand, and said, "Thanks, Mate."

"Okay, Gentlemen, let's call it a day, shall we?"

As Daniel and Timothy left the office, Ian asked, "John, what do you think about Mister Rawlins. Can he do the job?"

"Ian, I don't know. I think he can if he puts his mind to it. He understands the needs of a ship, which helps. I do know if it is too much for him, he will come forward to tell you."

FIFTY FOUR ✶

John and Rebeka purchased a house that had
become available because the owner moved into
a larger home that had been in the process of
being finished for the past year. The house was
detached, and did not have another one fastened
to either end. It was smaller than most of these
kinds of houses. Theirs was only two stories high
and it contained more rooms than John thought
they would ever use.

Katherine fell in love with the cottage the first time
she'd ever been inside those many months
before, and when she learned of Rebeka's wish to
have a house, the two of them started talking and
they'd come to an agreement while their
husbands had been away at sea. Both women
had been hesitant in the beginning. The decision
about the homes was something their husbands
would normally have the final say about. Still, they
both felt sure the men in their lives would do as
the two of them wished.

After the cottage had been vacated, Jim and
Katherine moved into it, and it was only a short
time before Katherine had committed herself to a
gathering in her new home.

She had sent invitations to all of the women in her
new social group, and she didn't know if any of
them would accept an invitation to a mere
'Cottage' get together.

She had gone even further, she stressed in her invitation that it was to be an informal gathering.

She was surprised when the first carriage arrived late of the morning for her planned party. From it alighted Jesselyn, Margaret's maid. When Katherine met her at the door, Jesselyn said, "Morning, Mum. Missus Davis sent some fresh vegetables from her garden and I'm to fix them for your party, Mum."

Katherine looked at her in awe, and Jesselyn knew the question on her mind without its being asked. "Rebeka arranged my day with you, Mum. Missus Hawkins gave her permission, and there's to be a carriage from her later, Mum."

"Oh, Jessie, please do come in, and thank you, and please, Jessie, no more 'Mum' talk, you know perfectly well what my name is."

She smiled as she said, "Yes. . . ahh, Katherine, if you'd be so kind as to help me bring in the vegetables from the carriage?"

After the two of them placed everything in the kitchen, Jesselyn took charge, and Katherine went on to her other preparations. Her mind reeled with excitement. *'Perhaps a few are coming after all!'*

It was not long before another carriage arrived. The footman knocked at the door, and when Katherine opened the door, he said, "I've a delivery, Mum."

Before she could say anything, Jesselyn came up behind her, and as she wiped her hands on an apron, she said, "You go about your business. I'll see to the deliveries."

"Deliveries?"

"Yes. . . .Katherine. There's to be more."

Katherine walked away, she would go finish her hair. It just seemed odd to have someone else do these things for her, and now she had no idea how many might attend her doings. She felt giddy and excited with the anticipation.

During the day, she thought there had been more carriages on her lane in one day, than it usually saw in a month. She noted during one part of the day that the neighbors were coming outside to witness how many had been passing, and the day was far from over. She was also aware that a great variety of pastries had arrived from Lissa Franklin.

Fine wines also had come from John and Rebeka, and more from Ian and Margaret. Richard had sent ice from his warehouse to keep many items fresh and cool, and Constance saw to an abundance of spices, though she didn't attend, as she was feeling ill.

Rebeka and John came just a few minutes earlier than the appointed hour of two of the afternoon. Jesselyn met them at the door, and Rebeka hugged her as she said, "Jesselyn, thank you so much for doing my work for me with the vegetables."

"My pleasure, Mum, and a good day to you, Mister Davis."

"Good day, Jesselyn."

"I believe you two know your way around the cottage, and can make yourself comfortable?"

Rebeka laughed, "That we can." It did seem strange to John. The cottage looked different to him now. Smaller, of course, but with Katherine and Jim's things inside, it was just not the same place he'd lived for a number of years.

Most of the guests had arrived in ones and twos, including Elizabeth Bellis, whom Katherine had met, but who was more of a social friend to Margaret and Ian. She turned as she heard yet another knock at her door, and when Jesselyn answered the door, and Katherine saw who it was, she moved to the door straight away.

Jesselyn had taken their garments and left the guests to Katherine. Katherine spoke first, "Captain Mathews, welcome to our humble home, and to your good wife. . . "

"Ah. . .yes. Missus Barnstable, this is my wife, Gwendolyn."

"Captain, you will find my husband and the other men near the windows. I'll look after Gwendolyn."

Daniel looked to his wife and she nodded an okay, then he departed to join the others. "Gwendolyn, I'm Katherine, you can call me Kate if you like."

The newest ship's captain's wife let out an audible sigh of relief. "Kate, please call me Gwen, and thank you for the invitation. I must admit I'm so nervous I don't know what to do."

"First off, make up your mind you belong here. After that it will get easier."

"That's an easy thought for you, but this is a much different world for me."

Katherine laughed loud enough that she had to cover her mouth. Gwendolyn looked on, though she did not see the humor in what she'd said.

Then Katherine explained, "Gwen, I've only just recently joined this group myself. But come along my friend and let me introduce you around to the ladies."

The first one she introduced Gwendolyn to, was of course, Rebeka. "Becky, this is Gwen. Captain Mathews' wife."

Rebeka put her cup down into the saucer, "Gwen, how nice of you to join us."

"Thank you. . . Becky."

Katherine said, "Becky, tell her how long you've belonged to this group of women."

Rebeka understood the reason for what Katherine had said, "It's been just over a year now, since John got his first command."

Gwendolyn was introduced to all of the other women in the cottage. She liked three of them more than the others. Katherine, Rebeka and Lissa Franklin. Now, Katherine took her to where the men stood talking ships and shipping, and they were sampling every bottle of wine in the room. Some would be showing signs of having had too much to drink later in the day.

When they stopped at the edge of the group, Katherine said, "Gentlemen, if you will? This is Captain Mathews' wife, Gwendolyn. Gwendolyn, this is my husband, Ships Pilot Jim Barnstable, here is Rebeka's husband, Captain John Davis; and here," she said as she lay her hand affectionately on his arm, "is Margaret's husband Captain Ian Hawkins. Turning slightly she continued, "This gentleman is Mister Richard Humphry, Constance's husband, and the man to whom we owe our thanks for his wonderful pastries, Mister Tom Franklin, Lissa's husband."

Each of them acknowledged her, with a polite, "Missus Mathews." She knew she would come to know most of them on a more personal basis over time. Before the two of them left the men, Gwendolyn tugged at her husband's arm, pulled him closer to her and spoke to him quietly. "Daniel, thank you for talking me into coming. It is wonderful."

Rebeka looked up as Gwendolyn and Katherine returned. When she did, her eyes caught sight of Captain Mathews. He mouthed a *'Thank you.'* to her. She smiled knowing his feelings. Katherine had not seen the exchange, but Rebeka would tell her later.

The last to arrive was Reginald Bowers and Katherine watched as Jesselyn met him at the door. He did not move into the room right away. Instead, he stood talking with Jesselyn. She wasn't sure, but she thought she saw Jesselyn blush, then smile. Katherine joined them at the door.

"Mister Bowers, I'm glad you could join us this fine day." She steered him toward the group of men, but he hesitated before reaching the others.

"Jesselyn is quite attractive isn't she?"

She turned to look at the young woman, "Yes, she is." Now she understood that
Reginald Bowers had made an advance on Jesselyn. During the remainder of the gathering in her home, she noted he spent a great deal of time staying close to Jesselyn.

After their guests had all gone on their way, Jim could not fathom why his wife was singing as she put their home back together and put things away. He didn't know why, but she seemed happier than normal. He knew he and the other men had a very nice day themselves. He also knew he was going to be employed with Humphry Limited for as long as he wished.

FIFTY FIVE ✫

Margaret was just passing time as she worked on a new needle work project. Her eyes broke away from the fine stitchery as the light knocking at her open sitting room door interrupted her thinking. "Jesselyn, dear. What is it?"

"I need to speak to you, Mum."

"Of course. Please, sit by my side." She picked up an assortment of threads from the chair next to her.

"Might I shut the door, Mum?"

This caught Margaret's attention, "If you like." This was to be a serious conversation.
Jesselyn settled in the chair. It was apparent to Margaret that Jesselyn was nervous about something. "What is it, dear child?"

"I've to beg your forgiveness, Mum."

"Jesselyn, you've done nothing to be forgiven for."

"I'm about to, Mum. I've come to tell you that I'm leaving your service at months end, Mum."

Margaret leaned back in her chair. Jesselyn had been with her for better than four years and had become one of the family. Margaret was fond of her and now shocked by her announcement.

"You're serious, aren't you?"

She smiled tightly, though still worried. "Yes, Mum."

"Whatever are you going to do?"

"It's Mister Bowers, Mum. I've grown fond of him and he treats me like a queen, Mum."

"Reginald Bowers is a wealthy man, Jesselyn. I know he is taken with you, but you must understand there are several years between your ages."

"He's offered me rooms above his place of business, and he's placed money in safe keeping for me. It's money that only I have access to with promises of more to come. I feel confident in him, and he loves me, I'm sure of that."

Margaret smiled, she was pleased for Jesselyn. "There'll be talk you know. Some of it will not be polite."

"I expect that, Mum."

"Jesselyn, I wish you well in your upcoming life style."

"And, Jesselyn. None of the idle talk will come from this household."

Jesselyn rose from her chair, "Thank you, Margaret."

"Jesselyn, one more thing."

"Yes,"

"I'll see to it that there is an extra months wages in your purse when you take your leave."

FIFTY SIX ✳

It was after two of the morning when Lissa shook Tom's shoulder. "Tom."

As he came out of a deep slumber, "What, what is it?"

"Tom, there's a noise at the back of the cottage. I didn't hear anyone knock, but I'm sure someone is there."

He rose up to his elbow. Then he too heard the noise, a tapping sound on one of the windows near the door. He turned up the wick on the oil lamp bathing the room in a soft golden glow of color. He stood and pulled on a night shirt then started for the back of the cottage. In the kitchen he looked out the window and could not believe his eyes. After he pulled the latch back to release the door so it could be opened, Lissa heard him speaking to someone.

She rose and, after putting on a night dress, she pulled her long hair back over her shoulder, then she walked silently to the kitchen. She stopped just outside the door and peeked inside the room to see whom Tom was talking with. Her fingers came up to her lips as she stifled a gasp at the sight. The man had little hair, but what he had was in a long braid down his back, his skin was weathered from years of sea and sun. His teeth, from what little she could see, were dark in color from abuse and lack of care. And his hand, when he saw her, and pointed to her, only had three fingers.

"Aye, Tom, me Bucko. That be your lady, there. She's a fine one she is."

Tom turned, then motioned for her to come. "Lissa, this is my old friend Three Finger Jack."

Lissa covered herself as best she could then moved to stand behind her husband. "Mister Jack." She replied."

"I can't stay, Tom. I'm a wanted man, and you two canny say I've been about. Should anyone ask, you've not seen me."

"Jack, what is it that brings you to my home at this hour?"

"I only came to bring you a gift, Lad. To repay a kindness you gave me at the mast."

"Jack, you needn't give me a gift for that, we were shipmates."

"You were more than that, Tom." He went to the door, reached down just outside, then leaving the door open on his return, he lifted the heavy leather bag and placed it on the table.

"Goodnight to you then." He brought his three finger hand up in a salute, "You've a fine wife there, Tom." In moments he was gone, the dark of night swallowing him like he'd never existed.

When he was gone Tom latched the door, and looked as Lissa lifted the bag. "It's quite heavy, Tom."

Tom took the bag from her, opened the draw stings and poured the contents out onto the table top. Gold coins covered the surface.

In the days that followed there were rumors of a dark ship having spent a night at anchor just inside the bay entrance. Some thought it to be pirates, but no harm had come to anyone.

FIFTY SEVEN ✶

Jesselyn provided them hot tea and a serving of cookies from Franklin's bakery. It was the latest delicacy they were devouring. The three men stood around a large table sipping from small delicate cups, and eating the new kind of pastry. Navigational charts were spread everywhere and each chart contained updated instructions on them in various places before the printing began.

Reginald Bowers was saying, "We've a fortune here, Gentlemen. These will find a ready market nearly anywhere in the world."

"That we do," William Becker replied. "But, it will make a ship's Captain's position as his own Navigator much easier, and it takes too long to train a Pilot."

"We'll still need to travel to keep them updated between each new printing. And, as we've discussed, we can offer a new free chart to any Captain who gives us news of his travels that we can use."

William asked Reginald, "You're sure the printer can handle these large prints?"

He answered, "Yes, he can. Let me show you a sample of his work." From under the table he withdrew a large rolled tube of paper. As he unrolled it, their eyes took in the details of their own Still Water Bay. The black ink print was done in great detail, but looked very professional. The heading along the bottom edge was printed in bold letters.

'THE PILOTS CHART COMPANY'

Jim Barnstable spoke up asking, "How long did it take to get this ready to print?"

"His engraver took nearly two months just to cut the lead plate. He told me he will have to hire a strong man just to move each one to the press every time we need new printings made of each chart."

Jim said, "Then we should make enough prints each time to last for a while."

William added, "We'll need to find a way to seal them against the water, and I've an idea on how we can do that."

Their first customer, Captain John Davis, was anxious to see their first printing. He wanted to use one of their charts on his trip to Portugal. Jim was to go along to see to any questions or corrections before they went into full printing production.

FIFTY EIGHT ✷

Phillip was packing his duffle while his mother watched anxiously. Though he was nine she felt odd about having him go to sea aboard the Quest for a voyage with his father. It was his intense curiosity that had led to this. Though he and his sister, Rachelle could read and write, it was Phillips constant search for knowledge that had led him to ask his father to take him on this voyage. His passion at the time was about ships and how they were built.

Rebeka went downstairs while he finished and she found John in the library sipping tea as he looked over his collection of books. He was looking for one or two to take with him this time. As she came to his side, he reached an arm around her pulling her against him. "Good Morning, Love."

She kissed him on the cheek, then said, "John, you keep a close eye on Phillip."

"He'll be fine, Rebeka. Don't worry."

"But John he wants to sleep in the fo'c'sle with the crew."

"Rebeka my crew looks at him as if he were their own blood and it was his choice to go forward."

*   *   *

As they left the harbour, he and Jim, the Pilot, were looking at the navigational chart Jim's company had provided. Jim was trying not to offer advice on their transit out of the bay. He wanted John to do it with the aid of the chart.

John stood at the bridgedeck rail looking forward, then down at his chart, then forward again. To his First Mate he said, "Mister Harmon, bring her a bit to the starboard."

"Aye, Sir." He repeated the order to the Helmsman. "Mister Swit, bring her one spoke to starboard."

"Aye, Sir. Starboard, Sir." His hands shifted one spoke further to the right on the large wheel. The ship moved slowly but came up to her new course. Then he kept her there.

Once they cleared land's end and the watches were set, he and Jim went below. As they looked over the remaining charts to be used for the entrance into Portugal, John said, "Jim these are wonderful charts. I thank you for their use."

"Ah, tis I who should be thanking you. We'll know when we've returned if they are worth the trouble and expense to make."

The trip to Portugal had gone well. A cargo of good Portugese wines and of the finest cheese rounds, filled the hold below. It was a cargo that would sell quickly in England.

*   *   *

They were nearing home waters as John watched his son, Phillip. He often spent his hours talking to the different hands aboard the Quest. They did not stop their work to talk to him because he was the son of the ship's captain. They stopped because they took an interest in his search for an understanding of all things about ships and the men who ran them.

His Bo'sun, Jim Hurley approached him at the bridgedeck rail, both men looking at the boy as he made the rounds of talking with the crew, "He's a pocket full of questions, Captain."

John smiled, "That he is. He drives his mother over the brink at times with his thirst for answers. He's old enough now that the things he asks her are things she has no knowledge of so she sends him to those who can give him the answers he seeks."

"Aye, Sir. Just this morning he asked me how many ribs the ship had in her hull. I had to tell him I had no idea."

Surprised, John stood up straighter. "He hasn't asked me that question."

"I don't think he will, Sir."

"Why not?"

" Seems it was something he wanted to know right then, Sir, then he counted them himself."

"Has he shown you his ship drawings?"

"Aye, Sir. His ships don't look like anything I've ever seen, Sir."

"Nor I, Mister Harmon."

"He's a smart one, that one, Captain. Ahead of his time, he is."

*   *   *

As Phillip dined with his father in the Captain's cabin that evening, he said, "Father, the ship is built wrong."

John was amused, "How do you know she's built wrong?"

"She's slow."

"She's large, she carries a large cargo, but for a ship this size, she is faster than most."

"I've watched you take her out to sea. You start with the Jibs and Spanker, then add the Mains'ls after she's gathered way."

"It works best that way most of the time."

"Why not just use Jibs and larger Spankers? They wouldn't be as much work for the crew, the ships would be easier to build, and they would go faster."

He made a good point, and John didn't quite have an answer for it. "We use the larger square sails to gather the wind on long voyages as there is more canvas up to carry us along."

Phillip sat quietly for a few moments, as he tore his bread apart eating each piece while he thought about what he was going to tell his father. Then, "Father, I want to build ships."

John had never really considered what his son might like to do with his life. He was still so young. "I suppose we could arrange for you to apprentice with a shipwright."

"Oh, no, Father, I don't want to build them myself. I want to tell the shipwrights how to build them."

FIFTY NINE ✶

As the Quest was being moored along side the wharf, John looked until he found Rebeka and Rachelle waiting in the crowd. He continued to look, but he did not see Ian and he had expected him, too. After the ship was moored properly, the end of the gangway was brought aboard the ship and those having business aboard were allowed on deck.

When she arrived, Rebeka was worried about her son, she missed him terribly while he was away and she was quick to ask, "John, where is Phillip?"

"He's in my cabin carefully packing the last of his drawings. Come, we'll go below." John picked up Rachelle, "Ahh my dear child, you are getting much too big for me to be picking you up like this."

"Yes, Father, I am. But I still like it when you do it."

He kissed her on the forehead then put her back down but held her hand as they went aft. With his arm around Rebeka's waist he pulled her close, and their hips pressed together. He broke the spell with, "I did not see Ian or Margaret on the wharf."

She stopped, held his hand and said, "Rachelle, you go on ahead to your father's cabin. We'll be right along."

"Yes, Mother."

When she was gone, Rebeka looked at John, tears forming in her eyes. "Ian passed away ten days ago."

"Oh, my God. Ian's gone from us?"

"Yes. His heart stopped and Margaret could not help him."

They stood quietly together for several moments until, finally, John said, "What's to become of Margaret?"

"She's a good friend, John, and I've thought about her a great deal. I've an idea, but we can talk about that tonight."

SIXTY ✶

It had taken a great deal of persuasion, but John and Rebeka were able to convince Margaret to come live with them. Over the years the children had grown fond of her and thought of her as the grandmother they never had. Their own grandparents were lost to the cholera epidemic many years past. When John asked Tom and Lissa, among many other friends, to help he and Rebeka move Margaret's things to their house, Tom and Lissa had asked Margaret to sell them her house. Because she would no longer have need of the large house she'd agreed. She was paid in gold coins.

Most of the community who knew Ian and Margaret had helped in the move. The Humphry Company warehouse wagons were used, and still it took two weeks and a couple of days to complete the move. The things that Margaret had not sold or given away still filled four rooms. The end of the house where she now resided, had its own entrance off her day to day living area, but she also had her bedroom, a room she used as a parlor, and one for a library, of which Phillip was especially fond. She took her meals with the family and helped with the lighter kitchen chores.

One afternoon after she'd settled in, Margaret took Phillip by the hand and led him through the library. She pointed out Ian's collection of books on ship building and design. He'd collected many volumes over time, all regarding ships and shipping. Phillip began to spend hours in her library reading and making notes and drawings.

One afternoon, she said to Phillip, "Phillip, I have a friend who owns the shipyard here in Still Water. He's agreed to accept you as an apprentice in his design office, if you would be interested."

The boy rushed to her, his arms surrounding her. His face buried against her bosom, he could only say, "Thank you so much! Yes, please yes!"

When she pulled him back to look into his eyes, she saw tears running down his cheeks. Then she pulled him close again. He soon rushed to tell his mother and father the news. They acted quite surprised, though Margaret had already asked their permission. In the coming weeks at the shipyard offices he began working with various woods and making model ships. His mentor wanted to see how his designs worked out in a water tank. Some who saw his creations thought them radical, but one fishing ship owner was very interested.

Rachelle, too, was taken in hand by Margaret. She was beginning to learn the finer points of becoming a young lady who was to be introduced into the social circles. Margaret had decided she would teach Rachelle how to be a proper lady so as to attract a wealthy young man when the time came. She was learning the finer points of etiquette and the polished ways of a lady who is well to do.

SIXTY ONE ✶

Before Ian's death, he'd discovered a few discrepancies in what the books said they had in the warehouse and what the man who kept track of the stock told him they actually had in stock. Ian had decided to hold a complete inventory of the warehouses belonging to Humphry Limited on the first of the coming month. Everyone who was connected to that part of the company was expected to help with the inventory when it took place.

Three days after he'd made the announcement about the inventory, the Quartermaster, Timothy Rawlins, was known to have arranged passage to France. It was not known where he was headed, just that he'd mentioned accepting a position elsewhere.

This seemed odd, as no one remembered his being able to speak anything more than bar room French. The reason for his departure was better understood after the results of the inventory were made clear. Seems Timothy had neglected to give the funds he'd received in payment, to Martin at the end of a business day. These were monies from a few trusted small ship owners who purchased items from the company.

Other books written by Donald Boone

Impact

Lost Island

The Investigator

The Sea Pilot

Those Still Alive

Welcome Aboard

www.ingramcontent.com/pod-product-compliance
Lightning Source LLC
Chambersburg PA
CBHW072219170626
46813CB00003B/1013